OUTNUMBERED

The corporal jammed the hammer of his Springfield back to full cock.

And Longarm's first bullet hit him square in the chest at the same instant.

The Piegan probably didn't even see the speed of the draw that killed him.

Behind the corporal, the rest of the police were trying to get their guns into action. One got a shot off . . .

DON'T MISS THESE
ALL-ACTION WESTERN SERIES
FROM THE BERKLEY PUBLISHING GROUP

THE GUNSMITH by J. R. Roberts
   Clint Adams was a legend among lawmen, outlaws, and ladies.
   They called him . . . the Gunsmith.

LONGARM by Tabor Evans
   The popular long-running series about U.S. Deputy Marshal
   Long—his life, his loves, his fight for justice.

SLOCUM by Jake Logan
   Today's longest-running action Western. John Slocum rides a
   deadly trail of hot blood and cold steel.

TABOR EVANS

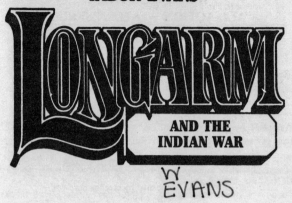

LONGARM

AND THE INDIAN WAR

W
EVANS

JOVE BOOKS, NEW YORK

LONGARM AND THE INDIAN WAR

A Jove Book / published by arrangement with
the author

PRINTING HISTORY
Jove edition / April 1997

All rights reserved.
Copyright © 1997 by Jove Publications, Inc.
This book may not be reproduced in whole
or in part, by mimeograph or any other means,
without permission. For information address:
The Berkley Publishing Group, 200 Madison Avenue,
New York, New York 10016.

The Putnam Berkley World Wide Web site address is
http://www.berkley.com/berkley

ISBN: 0-515-12050-2

A JOVE BOOK®
Jove Books are published by The Berkley Publishing Group,
200 Madison Avenue, New York, New York 10016.
JOVE and the "J" design are trademarks
belonging to Jove Publications, Inc.

PRINTED IN THE UNITED STATES OF AMERICA

10 9 8 7 6 5 4 3 2 1

LONGARM

AND THE
INDIAN WAR

Chapter 1

This was the day. The one Longarm had been dreading. They all knew it was coming, and they all damn well hated it. Unfortunately they had no choice in the matter, not Longarm and not any one of the other United States deputy marshals who worked under Marshal William Vail, head of the Justice Department's Denver District.

This detestable job was going to require the efforts of every man the marshal could put in the saddle, and even then it would take weeks to complete.

The problem, of course, was the United States Congress and its meddling committees. In this case the committee members—well, more accurately their staffs; the Congressmen themselves would only lend their hands to the effort when there was glory to be handed out—were investigating alleged profiteering and political kickbacks among the moneyed silver mining interests.

Big surprise if true. Sure it was, Longarm told himself ruefully as he made his way through the pedestrian traffic along Colfax Avenue not far west of the gold-domed State Capitol Building.

It was morning of the day he'd been dreading, and his gait was considerably slower today than normal.

The problem for Billy Vail's deputies was not the actual investigation that was about to take place. Congressional staff members would take care of all that.

The deputies' jobs would be to get all the damned witnesses subpoenaed so the investigating—or political grandstanding, whatever—could begin.

There were, Longarm and the rest of the boys had been told, literally hundreds upon hundreds of subpoenas to receipt and deliver. To hundreds upon hundreds of potential witnesses. Who might damn well not want to be found and served with these particular instruments. And who, even if they held still and docilely waited for service, were spread out over much of Colorado, New Mexico, Utah, Wyoming, and Montana.

Finding them all, serving them all, completing the paperwork on them all was going to be a daunting proposition. Or in simpler terms, this was gonna be a bitch.

The formal start of the massive campaign was scheduled to begin this afternoon. Every deputy Billy could claim was supposed to show up at one o'clock for final instructions and a bundle of subpoenas.

For some reason Billy had sent word to Longarm last night that his presence was required at nine, though, well in advance of the general meeting.

Hence Longarm was making his way along Colfax at roughly his usual starting hour.

He reached the gray stone edifice that was the Federal Building and bounced up the steps, pausing in front of the

2

glass panels of the double doors to check his reflection and make sure he was fit to present himself for duty. What he saw was reasonably reassuring.

Deputy Marshal Custis Long was a tall and rangy man, standing something over six feet in height, with broad shoulders and a horseman's lean hips. He had a craggy and somewhat wind-burned face, brown hair, brown eyes, and a massive sweep of brown mustache as well.

This morning he wore a dark gray broadcloth suit, a pale yellow vest, and his customary flat-crowned brown Stetson hat.

Beneath the coat could be seen a gunbelt that supported a large and much used Colt double-action .44 revolver set in a cross-draw rig. Not so obvious was the perfectly normal-looking watch chain that stretched across Longarm's flat belly. One end of the chain was attached to the expected watch, in this instance a key-wound Ingersoll of railroad quality. At the other end, however, the "fob" was in fact a brass-framed .44-caliber derringer, a device that Longarm on occasion had found more useful than a normal decorative fob.

Longarm made sure everything was more or less in order, smoothed the ends of his mustache, and reached inside his coat for a slim, dark cheroot, which he trimmed and lighted before going inside and making his way—he could have done it by now while blindfolded, he was certain—to the U.S. Marshal's office.

"He's waiting for you," Marshal Vail's prim and bookish clerk said without preamble.

"I'm not late," Longarm protested.

"I didn't say you were. Just that he's waiting for you. You can go in now."

"An' a fine good morning to you too, Henry. Forget to

3

shave under that ear this morning, did you?" Longarm hung his Stetson on the rack behind Henry, and managed to keep a straight face as Henry surreptitiously felt of his face, first on one side and then the other, to make sure there was no unsightly stubble there. Which there was not. Longarm enjoyed teasing Henry at times, but he also liked and indeed respected the mild-seeming little man. Henry's appearance was not forbidding, but there was a core of spring steel inside him and he had never been known to back down from anything duty required of him. And Longarm was convinced beyond doubt that Henry would throw himself in front of an oncoming freight train if Billy Vail needed him to.

"What's this about, Henry? How come I have to be here before everybody else."

"Because they're all going to hate your guts when they find out, that's why. Because the boss has a plum assignment especially for you. Because now all the other fellows have to deliver your batch of subpoenas along with their own. And because you seem to live a charmed life that keeps you from being overwhelmed with the boredom that is the bane and the curse of all the rest of us. That's why." Henry sniffed and pushed his spectacles higher onto his nose.

Longarm laughed. "Try again, Henry. You aren't gonna get to me that easy. No false hopes for me today, thank you."

"At the risk of repeating myself, Deputy . . . he's waiting for you. Go right on in whenever it's convenient."

"Thanks." Longarm tapped lightly on Billy Vail's office door and let himself in without waiting for a response.

Chapter 2

"I don't like this," Billy Vail declared. "Not even a little bit."

"Doesn't anybody in this office remember how to say good morning?" Longarm complained.

"I remember how," the balding, round-faced marshal said. "I just don't damned well feel like it at the moment."

"What has you so pissed off this early in the morning?" Longarm asked, hooking a boot toe behind the leg of a straight chair in from of the boss's desk and dragging the chair around so he could straddle it backward and drape his forearms over what was supposed to be the back of the chair.

"Meddling," Vail said. "Bunch of damned political upstarts interfering with my plans. My personnel. The assignments in this office."

"I don't know what you are talking about," Longarm told him.

"If I thought for one second that you did, Long, I'd kick

your butt so hard you could wear your asshole for earmuffs.''

"I don't suppose you'd care t' tell me—"

"I already told you. Meddling, that's what."

"But . . ."

"You know how much work we have to do over the next several weeks," Vail complained.

"That I do," Longarm agreed. "It's gonna be a real bitch."

"It would have been a bitch if I had everyone on the job to do it. Now it will be even worse."

"So why won't you have everyone available?" Longarm asked.

"Are you sure you don't already know? Are you *sure* you didn't have anything to do with this?" Vail picked up the "this" in question, a brown-rimmed yellow message form, and waved it accusingly in Longarm's direction.

"Dammit, Boss, I don't even know what that is. An' I won't know until or unless you quit your bitching an' get around to tellin' me what that thing is."

"This," the marshal grumbled, "is a request . . . an order actually, of course, but we aren't supposed to call it that when certain political appointees may be involved. A request that one of my men, a particular one of my men at that, be detached from service with the Department of Justice and placed at the, um . . . let me get this right. . . ." Vail peered intently at the paper for a moment, his lips moving slightly and his normally genial features contorted into a scowl. "Placed under direction, that is the word they used, 'direction,' of the War Department. Specifically, that this Department of Justice employee be placed under the direction of a Colonel L. Thompson Wingate at a certain, um, Camp Beloit, which military encampment is adjacent to the . . . let me see here . . . the Upper Belle Fourche Intertribal Agency. Wherever and whatever that is.'' Billy Vail grunted and growled a little more and threw the message form down onto a small pile of other papers lying on his desk.

"What you're saying," Longarm drawled, trying to sort out the boss's distress, "is that one o' your deputies has got himself conscripted into the army? Sort of?"

"You could put it that way."

"The poor sonuvabitch," Longarm said with considerable feeling.

"You would rather be chasing all over the Rockies with papers to serve?" Vail asked.

"Rather than have to play hey-boy to some smartass army colonel? Hell, yes, I'd rather hang paper than that, Billy. You know how I feel about having to wipe butt whenever some other fella decides to fart. I'd a whole lot prefer running errands for those Congressmen. At least the Congressmen won't be around looking over my shoulder all the time."

"Then it appears that both of us are doomed to displeasure in this matter," Billy said, "because you are the deputy I've been 'requested' to reassign."

"What the hell for?" Longarm blurted out.

"Actually, I'm not sure. The only thing this telegram tells me is that the Secretary of War has personally requested your cooperation from the Attorney General."

"Me?"

"You. In particular. By name."

"But Boss, I never heard of no Colonel, uh . . . what was that name again?"

"L. Thompson Wingate."

"Yeah. Him. I never heard of him. Nor of the camp where he's posted. Nor for that matter of any Upper Belle Fourche

7

whatsis. I never heard of any of this, Boss, so how the hell did I get involved in it?''

"Perhaps Colonel Wingate can explain it to your satisfaction. The only thing I know for sure, Longarm, is that you are to travel there by the quickest means possible and will report yourself for duty under his command at your earliest convenience. Which in army terms, if I remember correctly, means right damn now or maybe a little bit sooner than that.''

"Right away, Boss," Longarm said. "Just as soon as I finish tossing a coin to decide do I head north, east, west, or south in order to find this place.''

"The Belle Fourche River, Deputy Long, is—''

"Yeah, boss, I know where the damn Belle Fourche is. I was just . . . you know.''

"Uh-huh. One more thing, Longarm.''

"Yes, sir?''

"If you happen to finish this detached assignment within the next week or two . . .''

"You can count on me, Boss. You know that.''

"Count on you to do what, Longarm?'' Vail managed a smile for the first time since Longarm came into his office. It wasn't much of one, but it was a smile nonetheless. "You'd best get along now. On your way out see Henry about travel arrangements. I asked him to look into the situation and see what he could do to expedite your journey.''

"Right.'' Longarm stood and stifled an impulse to salute the marshal. He didn't think Billy would find the gesture all that funny at the moment. "I'll be back quick as I can," he promised. And then, grinning, he added, "Call it a day or two after the rest of the boys get done hanging paper for the Congressmen.''

"Just remember one thing, Long," Vail said in a serious tone of voice.

"Yes, sir?"

"You only have to kiss their asses if they're majors or higher. Captains and below you can get by with a pucker and some kiss-kiss noise."

Longarm pretended deep thought for a few moments, then nodded and said, "Right. Got it. Thanks, Boss."

"Get out of here, Custis. And good luck."

Chapter 3

Getting to a place he'd never heard of before proved to be easy as sliding on greased ice. When Longarm came out of Billy Vail's office, Henry had a suggested itinerary already prepared for him . . . in two simple instructions. Take the train east to Julesburg, then the Deadwood, Dakota Territory, stage operated by the Blackelder Express Company.

"From Deadwood you won't have any trouble at all finding transportation on to Camp Beloit. The army will be buying supplies locally, so ask around. Someone is bound to know how you can get there."

Longarm was amazed. On two counts. The first was that Henry had somehow figured out a way for Longarm to get there when he was no more likely than Longarm to have known in advance that such a place as Camp Beloit existed. The second was that Henry had *not* figured out the last tiny details of Longarm's travel.

"When does the next eastbound pull out for Julesburg?" Longarm asked.

"Relax. You have almost two hours to make it."

"Hell, that's time enough for me to go home an' take a nap."

"I have your expense vouchers here," Henry said, tidying the paperwork into a bundle and handing it across his desk. "You won't need any for your transportation, though. Blackelder is a mail carrier. Just show your badge, same as on the train, and you're entitled to free passage. And don't let some fast-talking ticket agent cheat you out of one of these vouchers."

"Henry," Longarm protested, his face a mask of utter innocence. "Would I . . . ?"

"Yes, you most certainly would. Indeed, you have in the past. Next time, Longarm, I will disallow payment and you will have to make up the expenditure out of your own pocket. Do I make myself clear?"

"Yes, Mother," Longarm said contritely. He tucked the vouchers, as good as cash once they were endorsed in favor of a merchant or vendor, into an inside coat pocket where they would be safe.

"One more thing, Longarm."

"Yes, Henry?"

"Be careful."

"Henry. I didn't know you cared."

"I don't. But it would be a nuisance having to train someone new. And you will be dealing with the army, after all. One never knows. . . ."

Longarm laughed and winked at the clerkish little man, then ambled out the door and right on out of the Federal Building. He had a train to catch and quite a lot to do beforehand.

11

•　•　•

He didn't see much of Julesburg. Not that there was so very much there that needed seeing to begin with, but this trip through he saw even less than usual. It was past dark when he arrived and before daybreak when he left. If the Blackelder Express Company offices hadn't been in plain sight in the same block as Longarm's hotel, he probably would have missed seeing the schedule board and slept through the daily pre-dawn departure. That would have cost him a full day. Although in truth Longarm was not sure just how much of a hurry he was in to reach this Camp Beloit and place himself under the command of some colonel he'd never heard of. He supposed it would be best to get this—whatever *this* was— over with. If he had to start it at all.

And so, yawning and hungry—the damned hotel restaurant hadn't opened for business yet and he did not learn about that nasty little inconvenience until it was too late to go off looking for an early hours' cafe—he presented himself in front of the express company office promptly at five o'clock in the morning.

The coach, a full-sized Studebaker with inside seating for fourteen and room for nine more on the roof, was already hitched and ready. The jehu was a lean man with gray in his mustache and brown tobacco juice in his beard. He had one off eye and a mean look in the other one. All Longarm cared about, however, was whether he could handle his rig. Everything else was superfluous.

A hey-boy took Longarm's carpetbag and his saddle with the Winchester attached and stowed them in the big luggage boot hanging off the ass end of the Studebaker.

"Careful how you handle those, son," Longarm cautioned when he handed his things over. "I have a telegraph key in

12

the bag, and it doesn't need to be bounced around.''

The truth was that the key could take pretty much anything short of a direct whack from a nine-pound sledge. Also in that bag, though, was a bottle of Maryland rye whiskey that would not be quite so durable.

''Yes, sir, glad to oblige,'' the boy said. And threw Longarm's gear in a high, looping arc that ended somewhere in the bowels of the luggage boot. Longarm winced, although he did not hear any telltale tinkle of breaking glass.

Longarm wandered forward to glance at the team. He liked what he saw there. They were a six-up, all large and sleek and nicely muscled. Their feet looked carefully trimmed and shod, and their manes and tails were tidy.

''You got sommat to say, mister?'' the jehu challenged, his eyes narrowing slightly while he shot a stream of tobacco juice just barely wide of Longarm's left boot toe.

''Yes, I do,'' Longarm said. ''Fine-looking team there. You take care of them right.''

The jehu grunted loudly. And tried to hold back the beginnings of a grin. Obviously the old boy liked being complimented.

Longarm decided to gild the lily a bit—after all, he would be more or less at this fellow's mercies for the next four days or thereabouts—and offered the driver a cheroot.

''Thanks, don't mind if I do. Gotta tell you, though. There won't be no smoking inside the coach. Got a lady riding this trip. Sensitive, she is. If you wanta smoke you got to ride up top.''

Longarm surveyed the horizon to the west, the direction any weather would likely come in from. The sky remained dark, but so far as he could see it was also cloudless and not threatening. "Thanks for the advice, friend. Reckon I'll ride there for a spell."

"Got your ticket, mister?"

Longarm showed him the badge instead. The jehu shrugged. "It's all the same to me. They pay me the same if I take ten passengers or twenty, so you go on up and pick out a soft seat. We pull out in four minutes sharp, an' anybody that ain't aboard can take it up with Toby."

"Toby?" Longarm asked.

The driver grinned. "He's the young pup handling the lines of the rig that leaves this same time tomorra morning. Go on now. Crawl up there or I'll leave you standing here just like I would a paying customer. Maybe quicker."

Longarm did as he was told and crawled right up there.

Not, however, that he could find a soft seat. There didn't seem to be any of those available.

Chapter 4

Breakfast was a box affair . . . for those who'd known to bring one along, which left Longarm out.

Lunch was two cents' worth of stale biscuits and a glass of buttermilk . . . for which he had to pay forty cents . . . served and eaten aboard a decrepit ferry as it pulled across the North Platte.

By supper time Longarm felt fairly sure that if he didn't soon get a meal in his belly he was going to embarrass himself by keeling over in a girlish faint.

Either that or he was going to drag iron and rob the fat man riding down inside the coach. The fellow traveled with an entire hamper full of goodies, and every couple of miles Longarm would see a well-gnawed chicken bone or an apple core or the like sail out of the window on the side where the fat man was seated. It was damn well frustrating for someone who no longer could remember the feel of food in his stomach and whose only solace was to smoke a cheroot every now and then.

Solace of a more substantial nature might have been available except for the fact that Longarm's traveling jug, that is to say his bottle of rye, was locked away somewhere in the depths of the luggage boot.

Along about sundown, though, somewhere north of the Platte and south of Chadron, they finally pulled into Moore's Station, where they would get a change of team and a hot meal. Longarm had been looking forward to this ever since the stagecoach driver told him about it some hours earlier. By this point hunger and anticipation had merged so that he was salivating as soon as the place was in sight.

"Twenty-five minutes to eat," the driver, Quentin Cooper, called loudly enough for all to hear. "Twenty-five minutes and then we roll on, with you or without you."

"Dammit, Quint, it'll take me that long just to load my plate. I'm that hungry," Longarm complained.

"That's fine by me, Custis. Stay an' eat as long as y' like. You can always take the next upbound coach tomorra."

"You're a solicitous old son of a bitch, aren't you?"

"Did you just say something bad about me there, son?"

"What? You mean when I called you a son of a bitch?"

"God, no, Custis. Everybody calls me that. And mostly they're right. What I meant was that other word you used. What was it ag'in?"

"Solicitous?"

"That's the one. Is that something bad?"

"Not really."

"Well, all right then." Cooper chuckled and set the hand brake on the big Studebaker. "I thought for a minute there I was gonna have to whup you." Down below the other pas-

sengers were already piling out of the coach and racing each
other for the privilege of reaching the dinner tables first.

"Good thing for both of us it won't be necessary," Longarm allowed. "Need any help with the team?"

"Naw. Thanks, but naw. There's a boy around here someplace to lend a hand. You go on inside before the others clean
the place out an' there isn't anything left for you."

Longarm didn't offer a second time. He hit the ground in
one leap, and the door to the relay station in about three more.
Lordy, but he hadn't been this hungry since Methuselah was
a pup.

Quick as he was, though, he'd been handicapped by having
to make his start from atop the coach while everyone else was
near to ground level. All they'd had to do was pile out and
commence running. By the time Longarm got inside he was
at the ass end of a line of folks waiting to get to the table
where the food was laid out. He figured ten of his twenty-five
minutes would be used up just waiting for the slow-moving
line to reach the chow.

More likely the first twenty minutes would be shot, he realized once the persnickety, nose-high, smoke-hating ma'am
came in.

While everyone else, which is to say all the menfolk, had
been running to establish the line, she'd been outside taking
her own sweet time about things. Primping, preening, whatever the hell it is that highfalutin women do to prepare themselves for their adoring public.

Now, drifting in well behind everyone else, she sailed
through the door . . . and right on to the front of the line as if
that was the only possible place she could be expected to put
up with.

Longarm quietly seethed while the woman took her time

about things, standing there and oh-so-slowly stripping off her ivory-colored, elbow-length traveling gloves one tiny finger at a time so she could handle a plate. She was in no damned hurry, that was for sure.

He might not have minded all this so much if at least she'd presented something interesting to look at. But while he'd been traveling with her since before daybreak—well, on the same vehicle as her if not exactly down inside there *with* her— he had yet to get so much as a glimpse of what she looked like.

A delicate blossom, he figured. Or anyway she must have believed herself to be. She was dressed ears to toenails in an oversized duster, and wore a hat with a brim wide enough to protect a span of oxen. The hat was hung all around with a thick netting that he hoped allowed her to peer out from, for it sure as hell kept anyone else from looking in.

Until she got her gloves off he couldn't even have sworn that she was white. Until then he hadn't seen a hint of skin. And thanks to the loose fit of the voluminous duster, he still had no idea if she was built like a barrel or maybe just a barrel stave.

Not that he particularly gave a damn what this female creature looked like.

What he wanted was for her to get the hell done so he and all the rest of the males in the crowd could get some hot food in their bellies.

But no, not Miss Priss. She had to examine everything. Take a utensil and poke and turn at a bit of meat, even a dab of mashed potatoes. Everything had to be peered at, pored over, and thoroughly considered. Then she might, that is *might,* consent to place a speck of the item onto her plate. And there wasn't anything, not any-dang-thing, bigger than would conveniently fit into the mouth of a pigeon. A young pigeon at that. When she finally was done, having already used up a significant percentage of the total time that was available to the passengers, she didn't have enough food on her plate to satisfy the hunger of a healthy earthworm.

Longarm was disgusted. Also famished. And all the more so when he finally did reach the food line mere moments ahead of Quentin Cooper's loud call, ''Outside, everyone. Drop your forks and move your boots, everybody as wants to make the next leg north. Stage leaves in one minute. You hear? One minute an' I don't wait for nobody.''

Longarm believed him. Dammit. He put the plate down, picked up two slabs of crumbling bread instead, and piled them thick with whatever he could reach. Including a molehill-sized heap of mashed spuds. At least a potato sandwich would put something hot and filling into his belly.

But he still would've liked to throttle that damned female for holding up the line on them all.

He built a pair of open-faced sandwiches big enough that he should have hired a helper so he could carry them, then turned and loped back out to the stagecoach.

It was just coming dark when Quint snapped his whip above the twitching ears of his leaders and the big coach rocked and lurched into motion again.

Chapter 5

"Whoa, whoa there, goddammit!" The driver came halfway off his seat as he hauled and sawed at the lines, trying to drag the lumbering horses to a halt in time to avoid a man who suddenly appeared in the road before them. The man, who was afoot and seemingly alone in the middle of the night, was holding a lantern high, waving it from side to side. "Whoa, I said, goddammit."

Longarm reached under his coat and slid the .44 Colt into his hand, not making a big thing of it but intending to be prepared come whatever.

"Eddie? Is that you, Eddie?" Quentin Cooper called out. "Hold the light so's I can get a look at you. Be damned, Eddie, it is you. What the hell are you doin' out here on the road?"

"H'lo, Quint, it's me all right. I come to tell you the crick is over its banks. You won't be able to cross till the water goes down a good four, five feet."

"How come the creek to rise, Eddie?"

"Rainstorms somewhere upstream, I reckon. I dunno for sure, but the ford here is swimming deep to a giraffe. Eli tried to walk it this afternoon, tryin' to get the southbound across, but he like to drowned. Too much water running too fast for him to make it afoot. A coach and team would be swept away sure."

"Where's Eli now?" Cooper asked.

"He turned back. Said he'd take his passengers up to Howard Dancey's place to spend the night, an' asked me to wait here and tell you what was happening. Him and me figure you an' your people can sleep over at our place tonight. Maybe by morning you and him can make your crossing. Barring that, we can rig some ropes and swim across any passengers in a hurry. Then Eli can turn around an' finish your northbound leg whilst you take his people back south again. Depending on how the water is come daybreak, that is."

"Sounds all right to me, Eddie."

While that exchange was going on, Longarm returned the Colt to its holster and checked his pocket watch. It was ten before nine. Laying over for the night would put them behind schedule. Which was somewhat better than drowning, he had to admit. He stifled a yawn and pulled out a cheroot.

Looking at the bright side of things, maybe they could get something to eat at this farm or ranch or wherever it was they would be spending the night now. Longarm hadn't had time to fill up back there at Moore's Station, and a late supper would be welcome.

"I expect you all heard that," Quint shouted down to the passengers inside his coach. "We'll be turning off the road here and following this man for a half mile or thereabouts, then stop for the night." Cooper spat a stream of dark tobacco

21

juice in the general direction of his wheeler's hocks and added, "Just don't expect much in the way of accommodations. The Millers aren't generally in the business of taking in travelers."

Which, Longarm discovered shortly thereafter, was a truth and then some.

Eddie Miller's place was a homestead. Barely. There was a cabin made of warped and twisted cottonwood boles, a three-sided shed, a rickety little crapper just about big enough to turn around in, a small corral, and a root cellar in the dugout that presumably had been the initial dwelling place on the claim.

Miss Holier-than-Thou naturally enough assigned herself the relatively comfortable sleeping possibilities inside the cabin with the Millers. The men would have to make do as best they could under the shed roof or wherever else they might find a soft spot to spread their blankets on.

"Miz Miller has some coffee and hoecakes cooked up for us," the jehu announced before everyone scattered in search of sleeping space. "She has it laid out on a table on the porch over there, and she said she'll do what she can to put out a breakfast for us all come morning. She's a Christian lady, she is, an' won't take pay for being neighborly, but boys, if I was you I'd volunteer some little something by way of a thank-you for her trouble. And for the supplies she's using up on us when she could be feeding her own with it."

Longarm cooperated with the driver by taking off his own hat and passing it around. "None of that pale metal now, fellows," he chided those who would have tossed silver into the Stetson. "If it ain't yellow, then it better fold. You know what I mean?"

By the time everyone was done pitching in there was

22

enough in the hat to feed the Miller family for the next month. Which seemed fair enough.

Once again, though, Longarm found himself at the ass end of the line when it came to choosing a place to sleep. By the time he'd taken up the collection and passed it along, all the available floor space under the shed roof was long since claimed. Longarm shrugged and carried his bedroll out past the corral on the theory that at least out there he wouldn't have to put up with Fat Boy's snoring. If that man could snore as good as he could eat, the inside of that shed was certain to sound like it had locomotives rumbling through it the whole night long.

Longarm sat for a few minutes admiring the stars and munching one of Mrs. Miller's corn cakes, then loosened his clothes—but didn't remove anything save his hat—and stretched out with his old McClellan saddle for a pillow. It wasn't like this was anything new or strange to him. He'd slept in similar fashion many and many a night before this one.

It was a pretty enough night, but Longarm didn't stay awake to think about that.

He was asleep within seconds of letting his eyes droop closed.

He felt . . . shitty. He hadn't been asleep half long enough to feel rested and he resented being awakened. His face felt like someone had coated it with a lining of soft lead, and his head felt like that same someone had pumped it full of some thick, viscous liquid. Syrup or molasses. Or worse. His head ached and his throat was full of phlegm and all he wanted was to go back to sleep.

But someone was walking around mighty close by, and he

didn't know who it was or what they might be up to, and he damn well wasn't likely to fall asleep again until or unless he knew he was alone.

The footsteps came nearer and nearer yet, and he could hear the low murmur of voices kept deliberately soft. One male voice and one female one.

Well, that made sense. Of a sort. Sure enough, the two of them came close enough that he could get a look in the moonlight. It was Miss Priss—he could tell by the duster she wore and the wide, floppy-brimmed hat—and one of the men from the coach. Which one of those didn't hardly seem to matter.

Longarm only hoped they weren't going to get around to having their fun where they stood right now because that was only ten feet or so from where he'd laid his blankets and the situation could turn embarrassing. For all parties concerned, him included.

Shit, if he couldn't get laid himself, he didn't want to have to lie here and listen to someone else grunt and huff. If it came to that, he was thinking, maybe he should cough or pretend to snore or something to warn them off before things got serious.

The voices became a mite louder, although still not loud enough for him to make out any of the actual words. Which was just as well. He didn't particularly want to listen to some other fella's romantic lies to a traveling stranger.

Then the softness of the talk was shattered and the woman's voice turned hard.

"Damn you!" she snarled. "How *dare* you." Her hand swept up in a quick, unexpected slap that caught the male square across the chops and rocked him back onto his heels. Little Miss Lah-De-Dah had one helluva right when she wanted to uncork it.

"Hey!" the man barked, and his right hand flew high over the woman's head.

It was one thing to sit quiet and try to avoid intruding one someone else's moonlight tryst. It would have been something else entire to sit there and watch a grown man batter a woman. Any woman.

Longarm sprang off his bedding and was onto the man before the fellow had time to see him coming.

Well before the man's hand came down in a blow, Longarm planted a fist slam onto the bridge of his nose.

Apart from the force of the blow, which was considerable, Longarm had the advantage of surprise. It must have seemed like some avenging ghost was attacking out of the night. One moment there was only the couple standing there alone. The next second there was a malevolent presence added to the game. One that could punch like a mule can kick.

The man went down, rolled over and over through the dust, and came up to one knee with both hands pressed to his face. "Jesus, mister, you didn't have to do that," he complained.

Longarm wasn't much interested in starting a debate, so he kept quiet.

"I think you broke my nose," the fellow complained.

"I can bust more'n that if you want."

"Shit," the fellow mumbled, coming to his feet.

Longarm took half a step backward, readying himself, but there was no fight in the man in front of him.

"You want her, mister? She's yours." With that the fellow wobbled onto his feet, swayed a bit, and once he'd righted himself, stumbled off in the direction of the shed where the others were sleeping.

Longarm was left alone in the night with the imperious mystery woman.

Who, he noticed now, had removed her big hat and was standing now all wide-eyed and breathless in the pale moonlight.

She was, he saw, an uncommonly handsome creature with huge, intense eyes and hollow cheeks, both of which seemed to emphasize the generous size and full-lipped shape of her mouth.

And why was it, Longarm asked himself, that he was standing there staring so long and hard at those large, luminous eyes and, most especially, at the moist fullness of those lips.

He ought to say something, he decided. Introduce himself. Something.

Too late for the social niceties.

The woman stepped forward. Reached out to him.

For an instant Longarm felt like a hatchling fowl mesmerized into stony immobility by the cold gaze of a hungry snake.

Then the moment was past, and he felt the heat of the woman's breath enter his stunned and gaping mouth.

Chapter 6

Longarm surely did like it when a lady was willing to show appreciation for a gentleman's favor.

And lordy, was this woman ever appreciative.

First thing, she did her level best to suck his tongue smack out of his mouth. She tried and tried, and when it didn't work tried a little more.

And while her mouth was occupied with trying to swallow his tongue, her hands were just as busy peeling him out of the clothes he'd already loosened in anticipation of sleep. By the time she was done, Longarm had a pretty good idea of what an ear of fresh corn felt, like when an Iowa hausfrau was through shucking it. She'd peeled him as slickly as slipping the shell off a boiled egg.

Once Longarm was down to the buff, she went to work on herself. That was somewhat less of a trick since it turned out all she was wearing was that big floppy hat and the linen duster buttoned high to the throat. No doubt as a concession to modesty.

And all the while as she was tossing articles of clothing to each of the four sacred winds, she was somehow able to maintain her lip-lock on him. She did it all—he'd have sworn to it in a court of law if called upon under oath—without once having to break her kiss.

If, that is, so avid and passionate a contact could be called that. The term "kiss" did seem almighty tame when he considered the extent of what this gal was doing.

It was more like a rape or a ravishment than a simple kiss.

And all he was doing was standing there and taking it. She was the one doing all the work.

Within seconds—or minutes, he wasn't entirely sure and did not care in the slightest—the both of them were stark naked with the woman trying to crawl inside his mouth—another quarter inch or so and he figured she would bump into his tonsils and have to either give up where she was or hunker down to duck underneath them—while she simultaneously attempted to wrap herself so tight around him that she could swallow him whole.

All of which might sound a wee bit uncomfortable, but in fact was not.

The truth was that Longarm had no grounds for complaint here. Not at all.

This female carnivore was giving better than she got, and Longarm's reaction was a hard-on so intense it was a wonder it didn't draw blood from where it was poking her in the belly.

After a bit she backed off from his mouth long enough to grin and say, "Wow," as she reached down between them and felt of his cock. "You're hung like a fucking horse, honey."

And this was the delicate and fastidious little ol' thing that couldn't stand to be around a whiff of cigar smoke or wait ten seconds to be fed?

Some lady. Sure. You bet.

She was, however, one hellacious fine mouthful of a woman now that he could get a look at her. All of her.

She had a face that would have looked right at home carved in ivory and set onto a cameo, she was that pretty, with full lips and carefully groomed blond curls and prominent cheekbones emphasizing the slender hollows of her cheeks and neck.

Her body was built for speed more than comfort, its lines long and lean. Her belly was flat, and he could see each rib beside the small, pale saucers of her tits. Her nipples were tiny, pink, and pointy. She had a very small patch of blond hair at her crotch, and a pubic mound that was rounded and plump and pouty.

Her waist was small enough that it looked like he could span it with his hands, and her ass was so slim it should have looked boyish . . . except there was not one damned thing about this woman that could be considered in any way, shape, or form to be boyish or remotely masculine. Nothing. She was all female. Predatory female. And if he didn't take her on his own terms and mighty soon, Longarm felt reasonably sure, she would have her way with him and then, once done, spit him out.

What the hell, he thought. Better not take any chances with such a possibility.

He grabbed her, picked her up, and carried her the few steps to his bedroll.

She didn't offer objection. Not then and not when he knelt and laid her down onto the blankets.

The woman spread her slim thighs open wide in sheer invitation. Then she amplified that invitation by grabbing hold of his cock, still hard as marble if somewhat warmer, and pulling him down atop her.

Longarm didn't mind. He let her guide the way as his spear found a wet reception, and he plunged deep inside her.

The woman cried out, and for a moment he thought he'd hurt her. He was, after all, built somewhat bigger than most—or so he'd been told—and might have been difficult for her to accept.

It wasn't that at all, though. Her cry was pure pleasure. She wrapped her legs tight around him, her heels digging into his butt and urging him deeper and deeper still into the heat of her body.

She clung to him with both legs and both arms, and bit his shoulder for good measure. He doubted he could have shaken her off if he'd wanted to. Which he damn sure did not. This woman was as wild a ride as any bronco. And felt considerably better than one while he was in the saddle.

She squealed and gasped and thrashed her hips with mad abandon, and within seconds he could feel the tight, hot contractions encircle the base of his cock as she reached her first climax.

"Yes, yes, yes, damn you, yes," she encouraged, her breath hot in his ear and her pussy even hotter on his pecker. "Hard now. Fast. That's right."

He beat hell out of her with the flat of his belly, but she didn't complain about the abuse. Her response was to increase the tempo of their joining, raking his back with her clawed fingers and slamming him with her pelvis, thrusting upward with all her strength to meet his every downward stroke so that their coupling was fast and furious. "That's right, damn you. Do it; do it; do it."

He did it. She did it. And he was downright positive he felt her climax at least twice more, maybe three times, before his own ejaculation arrived, squirting hot fluids that he thought, hoped, would never quit. Damn, it was fine.

And when he was done, when he thought they were done, the woman laughed and slid out from under him and without so much as pausing to take a deep breath threw herself face-down on top of him, her mouth gulping and slurping, hot on his dripping cock, as she licked away the lingering drops of his semen and then took his cock into her mouth.

"Don't just lie there, damn you. Don't you know what *soix-ante-neuf* is?"

"Something to eat?" he asked.

She laughed. "Actually, it is. Sort of. No, stupid, it's French. It means sixty-nine. And—"

"I know what sixty-nine is," he told her.

"Oh?"

"Sure, it's what comes between sixty-eight an' seventy." He tugged a lock of pubic hair, which she had conveniently placed in front of his nose, then poked her in the asshole. "This bein' sixty-eight, y' see, and this other spot here bein' seventy."

"Shut up, you bastard, and eat me while I see if we can't get another rise out of Harry the Horse here."

"Harry?" he asked. "I don't recall that it's ever been called Harry before."

"Harry the Horse, dear. That makes all the difference."

"I see."

"Good. Now be quiet and make that tongue useful for something more interesting than a lot of noise, will you?"

31

Which he did. And she certainly did her part and then some. She had the rare ability to swallow a cock right on through her mouth and on into her throat, completely immersing him inside her there.

And while she was busy doing that at one end, at the other she was shuddering and fluttering, her slim body wracked with convulsive spasms as she reached repeated climaxes under the influence of Longarm's tongue on the tiny button that was the center of her pleasure.

All in all this was not, he thought, the very worst night he'd ever experienced.

Later, an hour or more later, when he lay panting in the cool night air, his balls aching from overwork and his limbs weak with fatigue, after the woman had left him and gone back to the Miller cabin, it occurred to Longarm that he did not yet know her name.

Not that he really gave a damn. What he did care about, what he did hope for, was whether she would be going all the way to Deadwood on this run. Because if she was, there would be several more nights they would have to get through.

He could think of worse things a man might have to face.

Chapter 7

The breakfast Mrs. Miller put together was both leisurely and large. A good thing too because Longarm had a lot of refueling to do after the exertions of the night before. By the time he was done with his tenth hotcake—or thereabouts, not that anyone was counting—Quentin Cooper and Eddie Miller were back from examining the state of the flooded creek.

"All right, everybody. We pull out quick as we're hitched and ready," the driver announced. "If you haven't already et, then you're too damn late. Let's go."

The creek, running far over its banks the night before, was narrow and placid in the morning light. Except for some mud left behind on the trunks of nearby trees, one would never think this little bit of a thing could be a bother to anybody. Which only went to prove one more time, Longarm thought, that looks can deceive.

They rolled north just half a day's run ahead of the trailing northbound that would have left Julesburg twenty-four hours behind them, changed teams at Darien's Gap, and left the fat man and three other passengers at Chadron that evening.

Longarm felt relieved. He'd been worried about the fellow lest his food hamper come empty and the poor soul not know how to handle the deprivation.

The woman—who Longarm hadn't had reason to so much as speak to the whole day long—remained with the coach.

To Longarm's surprise she not only stayed aboard, but when they filed onto the Studebaker after the supper stop, she clambered awkwardly onto the roof to sit up there in the cool evening air.

"Gonna be breezy up here, ma'am," the jehu warned. The woman nodded rather than bother her regal self by speaking to a peasant.

"The gentleman there smokes a cigar time to time, ma'am," Cooper added. "I can't hardly ask him to not smoke in the open air like this even if it bothers you, ma'am."

Again she nodded. She'd heard what the man had to say anyway.

"Bumpier up here too, ma'am. The rig kinda sways an' rocks so you feel it more than when you're down inside."

"Thank you. Drive on now." She flicked a finger in the direction of the road that led north.

"Yes, ma'am. Whatever you say, ma'am." Quint gave Longarm a slightly nervous look. Obviously he didn't want either the deputy or the fancy lady registering complaints with the stage line once they reached Deadwood, and this matchup appeared about as compatible as fire and gunpowder. Then, with a barely visible shrug, he consigned the problem to the fates and cracked his whip over the ears of his leaders.

The woman was no chatterbox, and didn't seem much interested in the scenery either. She sat—swayed, bumped, and bounced was more the truth of it—in unmoving silence until it became dark and for several hours after.

Until, that is, the next change of team. A quick stop to pour coffee in one end and pee out the other, and they were under way again.

And the woman again chose to ride on top of the big coach, although this time she took a seat facing the rear.

Liked to look at billowing dust, Longarm figured. At least that is what she would have been able to see had there been light enough to see anything. As it was, it had to be the horses that were keeping track of the roadbed, because it was entirely too dark for human eyes to make out anything.

Apart from the simple fact of it being black night, there were clouds to the north and west, and the moon was not yet showing to the east.

Longarm settled into his usual front-facing bench immediately behind Quentin Cooper so the two of them could chat if they took the notion—less likely than usual with a lady's tender ears so close—and pulled out a cheroot.

He hadn't any more than finished his smoke when he felt a sharp tap on his elbow. It was the woman, of course. She held a cautionary finger in front of her veil about where he expected her lips would be, then patted the seat beside her to indicate he should move back there with her.

Longarm took a look forward, but Quint was paying no attention to his passengers. And he shouldn't be, either, on a night so dark. One misstep by him or his leaders and the stage could bust a wheel, which would be a damned nuisance if not exactly a disaster. There were at least two spares slung underneath the body of the coach, but it was a bitch to jack a heavy coach off the ground and wrestle a new wheel in place. The chore would be especially annoying if it started to rain, and Longarm guessed by the clouds ahead and the smell of the air that they were likely to be rained on before morning.

Anyway, the driver was concentrating on what was in front of him and not what might be going on behind his back. Longarm nodded and shifted to the bench at the lady's side.

Again she motioned him to silence. Then she took his hand and slid it inside her duster, guiding it between two buttons.

And onto bare flesh.

Damned if she didn't seem to be naked again under that cover of heavy linen.

He goggled just a bit at the discovery. Then he felt around some to verify that, no, there wasn't any cloth anywhere to be found inside that garment. There was nothing but warm, soft skin.

The woman's head bobbed just a little, and despite the hat and veil Longarm was pretty sure she was laughing. She was enjoying this little joke, and probably had been the whole time, sitting there close by, naked as a boiled egg, and him never suspecting it.

Longarm chuckled too, and tweaked her nipple.

He heard what he thought to be a slightly muffled gasp. Then damned if she didn't reach over to his crotch and commence undoing buttons there.

Now there wasn't any way in hell the two of them could get away with fucking on top of a stagecoach full of folks traveling through wide-open country. Not even at night would anyone be crazy enough to try that. Not with Quint just a few feet away driving his team. Jeez!

They couldn't fuck, and it would have been a dead giveaway too if she'd gone to her knees in front of him.

It turned out what she had in mind was, in fact, safe enough from discovery to be worth a try.

She took him out of his britches and calmly, methodically, very gently, began to whack him off.

It was almighty considerate of her, Longarm thought. He leaned back and let her have her fun, a big part of which no doubt involved the risk of discovery and the very public experience of it all.

This odd woman just plain liked getting it on, it seemed.

Longarm did not complain once he reached that conclusion, just kinda enjoyed it while he could.

At one point she leaned close to his ear and in a barely audible whisper told him, "When you're about to come, signal me by squeezing my tit. Hard."

He nodded. At the appropriate moment he squeezed. Hard.

The woman gasped again, turned her head to check on Quentin Cooper, and then bent low, sweeping her veil aside and taking Longarm's cock into the wet heat of her mouth.

That was all he damn well needed to send him spilling over the edge. He came a quart. Hell, maybe more. Felt like that much anyway. And the woman drank it down without a murmur.

When she sat up again she was smiling. She winked at him and, silently laughing, licked her lips.

She carefully tucked him back where he belonged and buttoned his fly over the now-quite limp and satisfied appendage.

Then she took Longarm's hand and guided it down into the soft, furry nest of hair at her crotch.

This time she whispered, "Now me, dearie. Use your fingers. Deep and hard, honey."

This was, Longarm thought, a service every stagecoach line should lay on for its passengers. A man could make a fortune that way. Or a woman.

37

Chapter 8

Quentin Cooper had managed to make up almost three hours of their delay back at the Miller place, but the driver was grumbling and cussing himself for running behind schedule when they pulled into Deadwood late at night. They arrived in the middle of a rainstorm so heavy Longarm had been forced to abandon the coach roof and take shelter inside with the other passengers. The woman—she wasn't any lady—had had Cooper stop and let her get inside at the first hint of rainfall.

Which Longarm had found to be something of a relief. The damned female was insatiable. Hell, even atop a bumping stagecoach in the middle of the night, she'd been after him and after him until he thought his fingers were going to purely wear down to nubs. Then what would he do if he needed to shoot somebody. Or something. Why, the woman was practically dangerous. All in all he was just as happy to see the trip come to an end so he could forget about her and get on with business.

He did, of course, help her out of the coach and onto the covered sidewalk where a boy—her son? Longarm didn't know and wasn't told—showed up to take her luggage away.

Longarm's gear was the last to be unloaded. Naturally. He sometimes thought there was a Law of Nature to that regard. Or did it just seem that way?

"Thank you, Mr. Cooper. I enjoyed bein' in your charge these past few days."

"Don't tell me, son. Tell the boss."

"I'll make a point of it," Longarm told him, taking out a pair of cheroots and offering the spare to Quint.

"Thanks. Mind if I give you a word of advice?"

"Not at all, Mr. Cooper."

The jehu grinned. Big. "If you want to keep on doing what you been doing the past couple nights, son, you oughta learn to control your breathing. Times there you was grunting and snorting louder than my old Aunt Matilda." Cooper's grin got even bigger. Which Longarm would not have thought possible. "God, that woman can snore. Uh, my aunt, I mean. Not . . . you know."

Longarm laughed. "Mr. Cooper, I maybe shouldn't ought to tell you this . . . but it wasn't me doing that snorting."

"Oh, my. In that case I apologize, son. Forget I said anything."

Longarm struck a match and lighted Quint's smoke first, then his own. "Do you happen to know if there's a line that serves Camp Beloit or the Upper Belle Fourche Intertribal Agency? Whatever the hell that is?"

"No scheduled service that I know of, but Jess Maxwell at the general store two blocks down"—he pointed—"does business with them. You could talk to him about catching a ride out the next time he goes.''

"Thanks, Quint.''

"Jess won't be open till morning, of course. Meantime, you'd best avoid the hotel yonder and have a word with Mrs. Batson at the boardinghouse up the street there. She don't usually let rooms for one night at a time, but she'll take you in if you tell her I sent you. Her place is clean and cheap and you won't be woke up by a bunch of drunks.''

"Again, thanks.'' Longarm told the friendly driver good-bye, and shouldered his carpetbag and saddle, then ambled up the street in the direction Cooper indicated, a stream of cold rainwater pouring off the brim of his Stetson so that he had to be careful not to get the coal of his cheroot under the flow.

"Nope,'' Maxwell said curtly. The storekeeper was busy arranging stacks of ready-made flannel shirts on a shelf. But he didn't seem *that* busy.

"You mean no, you won't let me catch a ride? Or no, you—''

"What I mean, friend, is no, I won't be sending a wagon out there again.''

Longarm's belly growled hollowly, but he ignored it. He hadn't wanted to take time for breakfast this morning lest he risk missing his ride. Now he regretted that decision. It seemed he was not to have either breakfast or a ride. "Sorry,'' Longarm told Maxwell. "Quentin Cooper told me you do business out there.''

"Quint didn't lie. I did do business with the agency and the Beloit sutler too. But not no more. That's why I can't give you a lift, mister. I got no reason any longer to send a wagon out there.'' He finished with the shirts and bent over to open

another bale of merchandise, this one turning out to be a se-
lection of heavy-duty canvas trousers with woolen leggings
from the knee down, the sort of thing that would appeal to
placer miners who have to spend long hours wading in cold
creeks. "Anything else I can do for you?"

"I'd like to see what you have in the way of cigars. Cheroots like this one here if you have any."

"That I can help you with." For the first time since Longarm came in Jess Maxwell managed a smile.

"Three dollars a day," the livery stable hostler said. He spat
behind the heels of the animal he valued so very highly, a
mule with hams like a housecat and a tail no bigger around
than a pipe cleaner.

"Three dollars!" Longarm said. "For three dollars I can
hire a man."

"Mister, if you want to hire you some Cousin Jack to carry
you around on his shoulders all day, it's fine by me. And I
agree you can get you one for three dollars. But you'll pay
me three dollars if you want to put a saddle on something and
ride."

"It isn't even a horse, dammit."

"You got any idea how little call there is for saddle horses
around here? Or how much for mules? You're just damn lucky
that one of my mules happens to've been broke to saddle when
I bought it, or there wouldn't be anything for you to hire short
of a buckboard. And for that you'd pay five dollars a day. So
tell me . . . you want to rent my mule? Or go look for a Polack
to carry you piggyback to wherever you want to go?"

"Reckon I'll take the mule. But at two-fifty a day if I keep
him a week or longer."

"Three dollars."

"Two-fifty."

"Two-seventy-five. Starting the eighth day you have him. Three dollars until then. That's as low as I'll go."

Longarm grunted. And frowned.

The liveryman smiled. Hell, he ought to, Longarm thought. "Here, mister. Let me help you with that saddle. And to show you my heart's in the right place, I'll toss in a breastplate and crupper at no extra charge."

"You're a regular prince, you are."

"Yeah, everybody tells me that." The fellow whistled happily as he went about his work.

Chapter 9

Camp Beloit was . . . incomplete. That seemed the most charitable way to put it, Longarm decided. It would have been somewhat more accurate simply to say that the place was the asshole of the territory. But that would have been unkind.

Besides, he was not entirely clear on just exactly which territory Beloit should be considered the asshole of. Dakota? Montana? Wyoming? Longarm didn't know, and in truth did not much care, where the various lines were drawn. His interest was in why in hell he had been summoned to this . . . *place*.

Beloit seemed mostly to be made of mud. Wet, sagging, slippery mud. About two more good rains, Longarm figured, and what little there was of it would slide down into the creek that ran through it and disappear. Which, everything considered, might be a very good thing indeed.

From the foot of the broad, shallow valley where Longarm

sat on his rented mule and took in all the wondrous sights of Camp Beloit, there was damn little to see.

He could make out the sod roofs and smoke holes—nothing as fancy as chimneys or stovepipes for the poor sons of bitches who had to live here—of a dozen or more dugouts that had been gouged out of the hillside.

Two graying, mildewed, ratty tents sat at the head of a more or less level spot close by the creek.

And before them, not exactly grandiose or inspiring, was a crooked and twisted tree trunk that would best have served as firewood, but instead was being used as the garrison flagpole.

At the moment, presumably due to the fine drizzle that had been falling most of the morning, the flagpole was bare of its colors. Longarm considered that to be something of a blessing. He would have been embarrassed if he'd had to witness the desecration of a grand old flag by its presence above Camp Beloit.

Still and all, there was work to be done. He clucked softly to the mule and squeezed it lightly with his knees, putting the patient little animal in motion again.

A soldier appeared in the entry to the larger of the two tents and stood there peering at the newcomer, so Longarm aimed the mule in that direction.

"Sorry, sir," the man said as Longarm approached. "No civilians allowed on the reservation, sir. You'll have to turn back." Longarm was close enough now to see he was a corporal.

"Thanks, but I'm here to report to a Colonel Wingate."

"Yes, sir, and you would be?"

Longarm told the corporal who he was.

"And your business would be?"

"Damned if I know, son. I was only told to report. Nobody got around to telling me why."

The corporal cracked a thin smile. "That sounds like the army all right, sir. Wait here a moment, please." He turned and went inside the tent, which was much more commodious than Longarm had thought when he saw it from afar. The tent was a good thirty feet long and probably twenty wide. From the back of the mule—he had not been invited to step down— he could not see how it was laid out inside.

After a few moments the corporal reappeared, this time with a tall, gray-haired officer at his side. The officer was wearing a captain's shoulder boards. "You're Deputy Long?"

"I am, sir."

"Thank God. Get down, man, and come inside. I've been most anxious for you to arrive. Corporal, take the marshal's uh, mount."

"Yes, sir, but . . . what should I do with it, sir?"

"Draw a set of hobbles from Supply, corporal, and put the marshal's, um, animal with the, uh, horses."

"Won't they fight, sir?"

"It should be all right, son," Longarm put in. "The mule probably won't hurt the horses too bad."

The corporal, who did not appear to know a whole helluva lot about riding stock, gingerly accepted the mule's reins and led the, uh, animal off in the direction of the dugouts. Longarm had no idea where the alleged horses could be found. Somewhere out of sight from the camp headquarters tent obviously.

"Excuse me, Captain, but I was directed to report to a Colonel Wingate once I got here. Do you know where I could fine him?"

The tall captain smiled. "I am Wingate, sir."

Longarm's eyebrows went up a notch or two.

45

"My colonelcy was a brevet rank during the war. Referring to me by that rank now is a courtesy, perhaps a misplaced one, by my fellow officers. Sort of like calling George Custer general, if you see what I mean. He had in fact reverted to his permanent rank of lieutenant colonel when he died."

"I see," Longarm said. And in truth he did understand. It was the army. That was grounds enough to explain almost any insanity.

"Come inside now, please. We'll get you dried off and warmed up a little. Would you prefer brandy or a whiskey, Marshal? Then we can talk."

"Whiskey would be fine, but . . ."

"Come along now. No sense standing there in the rain."

"Yes, sir." Longarm trailed docilely along behind the captain/colonel who seemed to be in charge of this testament to the efficiency of Uncle Sam's boys in blue.

Chapter 10

"Do you know an Indian named Tall Man?" Wingate was seated in a folding camp chair, legs crossed and with a drink in one hand and a cigar in the other. He seemed every inch the officer and gentleman despite the rough surroundings.

"Sure I do," Longarm said. "Assuming it's the same one anyhow. I suppose there's prob'ly dozens with that same name. The fella I recall is a Crow. No taller than any other Indian, though. Kinda stout built with wide shoulders and a bum leg. Is that the Tall Man you mean?"

"That sounds like him, all right."

Longarm nodded and took a swallow of the whiskey. It wasn't rye, but it wasn't rotten either. "He ever tell you how he got the gimpy leg?"

"No, he hasn't."

"I did that to him. This was a while back, you understand. We had what you might call an altercation, and he came at me with a war club. Helluva unfriendly thing to do, especially

47

for a Crow. They like to pretend they've none of them ever killed a white man. You know?"

"Yes, I've heard that about the Crow," Wingate agreed.

"Yeah, well, don't believe everything you hear. Not about the Crow or any other tribe. But there's worse than the Crow, I will give them that. Anyway, that time I'm talking about, Tall Man was willing to put the Crow on record as having killed a U.S. deputy marshal. Me. Which I took exception to. So I shot him in the knee an' dropped him before he could plant that war club in the middle of my skull. I coulda killed him, of course, and maybe shoulda, but once he figured out that I wasn't going to, he was willing to talk out our differences. Which turned out to be more a matter of misunderstanding and misinterpretation than real difference. We talked plenty while he was laid up healing, and I suppose you could say that we became friends. Or close enough to it that the difference don't matter."

"Interesting," Wingate said. "That explains at least part of the reason you are needed here."

"Just part?" Longarm asked. "What's the rest of it?"

"Other than the Crow Tall Man, I take it you also are acquainted with an Indian known as Cloud Talker?"

Longarm had to think that one over. Eventually, frowning, he shook his head. "Nope, that don't ring no bells with me."

"What about John Jumps-the-Creek?"

"Old Johnny Jumper? Sure, I know him. Sort of a shaman with a band of Piegan over in the Marias River country."

"That's the man all right, but his people are not in the Marias River country any longer. They are here at this agency now."

"Really?" Longarm shrugged and took another swallow of the whiskey. Funny thing, but each bite tasted better than the last one had. Damn stuff was aging and improving even as he drank it. But then whiskey fairly often showed that same tendency, he'd noticed.

"So are Tall Man's band of Crow," Wingate mentioned.

Longarm had started raising his glass for another sample, sort of by way of experiment to see if his theory was holding up. On that news, however, his hand stopped in midair as if suddenly frozen in place. "John Jumps-the-Creek's band of Bloods an' the Crow cooped up on one piece of ground, Colonel? Has somebody lost his fucking mind?"

"It's possible," Wingate conceded. "I . . . had already begun to think that it was poor judgment to put them together. Perhaps you can tell me why?"

"My God, man, you don't know?"

"Deputy, I am not an expert in Indian affairs. To tell you the truth, I am not even experienced as a field commander. I am a staff officer. A damned good one if I do say so myself. But my area of expertise has to do with logistics planning. That is something that I do very well indeed. Well enough to have earned me that brevet promotion during the war even though I was rarely close enough to the battle lines to hear the cannon fire. Then afterward I was given administrative duties in New Orleans and, more recently, in Washington City. Last summer, for God knows what reason . . . certainly I never understood it . . . I was transferred out here. I had to go find a map just to locate Dakota Territory. I'd always had the impression Dakota was somewhere in the vicinity of Arkansas. Not that I was sure of where to find Arkansas either, actually. So if you could explain to me just why these two bands of Indians mistrust one another . . . I mean, really, they are all Indians, are they not? All sort of, well, brothers, so to speak?"

"They're all Indians, that's true enough. But a lot of folks

49

seem to have the idea that one Indian is pretty much like another except for maybe a few differences in the way they dress or whatever.''

"Yes, that has always been my impression."

"It's common enough," Longarm said, "but a helluva distance from the truth. Most Americans think being an Indian is like being American, and while some Americans are from Ohio and others are from Vermont, they're all Americans together. And the Indians are called by these different tribe names, but are like they're from different states."

"Exactly," Wingate said.

"Colonel, saying a Crow is the same as an Apache because they're both Indians is like saying an Irishman is the same as a Chinaman just because they both have black hair."

"I don't get it."

"One tribe of Indians is about as different from the others as one European nation is different from another. Some of the tribes have alliances, it's true. And some even have a sort of kinship. The Piegans, for instance, are related to the Blackfoot. It would make some kinda sense to put Piegans an' Blackfeet together at one agency. They can understand each other when they talk, and they aren't so likely to fight. Nothing real serious, anyhow. But putting Piegans an' Crow together is like mixing charcoal an' saltpeter. You know what that does, don't you?''

"Of course. Those are two of the primary ingredients in gunpowder."

"An' that's my point. I mean, Colonel, pretty much all the tribes except the Blackfeet hate the Piegan. The Sioux get along most of the time with the Cheyenne and the Arapaho. The Snakes hate everybody except the Pah-Ute, an' the Utes hate most everybody. And your friends the Crow? Far as I can tell, Colonel, there isn't any tribe that *doesn't* hate the Crow. Christ, even the Comanche will put up with the Kiowa sometimes. But the Crow? Every other tribe wants to take Crow scalps.''

''These Indian tribes would actually fight with one another?'' Wingate asked.

Longarm smiled. He couldn't help it. ''Colonel, you really are a babe in the woods out here. These Indian tribes do practically nothing *but* fight. An' until we came along and gave them all a common enemy to hate, all they had to fight against was each other. Could be we'll turn out to be the salvation of the Indian race by giving them all a single purpose, by bringing them together against us or something. It will take time before anybody will know about that. But in the meantime, their whole history has been one of constant warfare. That's all their warriors do. Or want to do. They fight. Us, each other, whoever's handy.''

''So if the Crow and the Piegan become angry with each other . . .''

''They'll fight. Sure as hell, Colonel, they'll go to war.''

''I hope,'' Wingate said, ''you can prevent that from happening here.''

''Pardon me?''

''I have reason to believe, deputy, that Tall Man's Crows and the Piegan of Cloud Talker may soon declare war on each other. Unless you can stop them.''

Longarm set his whiskey aside and leaned closer to hear the rest of this.

Chapter 11

Longarm and Captain Wingate topped a small rise some dozen miles north of Camp Beloit, the morning sun giving off a pale, watery light through a filter of light clouds that extended from one horizon to the next. They were mounted on horses, Longarm's a small-boned chestnut that belonged to the battalion adjutant. Neither Longarm nor Wingate thought it appropriate for Longarm to make his appearance at so potentially critical a meeting while sitting a mule's scrawny back.

And critical this could be, Longarm was thinking after a worrisome night. The northern tribes had been fairly peaceful these past few years. At the moment the only lingering Indian troubles of any real scope or importance involved the recurrent Apache outbreaks far to the south.

But a reopening of hostilities in the north could be a disaster, not only for the Indians involved, but because of the potential that violence, once started, could quickly spread to include innocent civilians who were flooding now onto lands once closed to them.

All through the northern plains prospectors and miners were leading the way into raw new lands, and businessmen were close on their heels. Wherever customers had needs to fill and money with which to buy, there would soon be a storekeeper eager to supply those needs. And where there were storekeepers there would as quickly be teamsters, freighters, and express lines. Wherever there were people in need of food, there soon thereafter were bound to be farmers breaking new ground to the plow, raising hay for livestock, grain for both stock and people, vegetables for the market. The burgeoning new towns would be in need of pork and eggs and chickens for the soup pot or the roaster. Ranchers would put cattle onto the open plains to graze, and wolfers would come along to collect furs and bounties and at the same time make the land safer for the production of meat and hides.

Wherever people gathered there soon would be churches, schools, whores, newspapers, and lawyers.

And all of this, every bit of it, was threatened by the likelihood of hostilities between the Crow and the Piegan.

Worrisome? Longarm damn well reckoned that it was. He hoped to be able to talk some sense into Tall Man and into Cloud Talker. Whoever the hell he was.

Talk some sense, that is, once he fully understood just what it was that was going on here. It was a subject Captain Wingate had left deliberately unclear.

"Like I told you," Wingate said the night before, "I know much too little about Indians and their ways. Even having the facts, or believing that I do, I am simply not prepared to deal with the problem as, well, as these Indians see it.

"Perhaps you will be able to both understand and to advise

53

them, Deputy. After all, both of them asked for your counsel.''

''For me?''

Wingate nodded. ''By name. And each one of them came up with the idea independently. Neither knew of the other's request. I am positive about that. They aren't talking to one another at all, unless you consider taunts and war cries to be conversation. No, each of them mentioned your name without knowing the other was doing the same. That is why I got my wire off to the War Department asking for your assignment here.''

''Kinda odd, don't you think, since I never heard of this Cloud Talker with the Bloods. Tall Man I know, but not Cloud Talker.''

''Perhaps Cloud Talker will explain that when you see him tomorrow,'' Wingate suggested.

Well, now they were fixing to find out what the deal was here.

Or so Longarm hoped.

Because a whole lot of lives could be at stake. It would be bad enough if the two bands of Indians squared off and went to war with each other.

But it would be a disaster of far-reaching influence if their battles picked the scabs off old wounds and reminded the other tribes that warfare was the most honorable expression of their way of life.

There would be pure hell to pay if the smell of gunsmoke from this quarrel whetted the appetites of the other tribes and new outbreaks spread through the northern tribes.

The tribes already resented the continuing incursions of whites into the Black Hills and out on the vast grasslands of the north. With that resentment already strong, there was no telling how small a spark might lead to a giant conflagration or how many lives could be wasted in the battles that would follow.

This business between the Crow and the Piegan on the Upper Belle Fourche was damn-all serious, Longarm knew, and his hope was that it could be defused without harm to anyone. That was why he was anxious now to see his old friend Tall Man. And to meet the Piegan who called himself Cloud Talker.

Toward that end he gave his borrowed horse only the briefest of rests before motioning for Wingate to follow and pressing on toward the ragged collection of lodges that marked the Crow encampment.

Chapter 12

"Is this the whole Crow camp?" Longarm asked, surprised by how few lodges there were. The entire affair was strung out for no more than a half mile or so along Janus Creek, while the Piegan camp, off in the distance past the Crows, was several times that size. What Longarm could see of it. There appeared to be more beyond a far rise, but he could not be sure of that.

"Three hundred twenty males of fighting age," Wingate told him.

"And the Piegan?"

"Something over nine hundred. I don't have an exact count for them. They keep promising to give one, but never seem to get around to it. Not even to the agent in charge of issuing their rations." Wingate smiled a little. "Drives him crazy, let me tell you."

"That isn't anything personal, Colonel. Not with you nor the Indian agent either. The Bloods are simply like that. They like to keep a few surprises in hand. If they ever do give you a figure, it won't be accurate. And they could move the numbers in either direction, down so you won't think they're a menace, or up so you'll think them stronger than they are. The one thing you can count on is that they won't tell you the truth.''

"Call it three hundred on the one side, though, and nine hundred on the other," Wingate said, going back to the original point. "If they decide to go to war, I will have one hundred twelve soldiers, including officers, to control them."

"Jeez, they gave you a lot to work with here, didn't they?" Longarm said.

"Two understrength companies of infantry. No field artillery. No field surgeon. No battalion stores. We are supposed to draw rations from the agency here. Military equipment, ammunition, and the like are to be requisitioned from Fort Robinson and hauled by civilian contractors. Which in practical terms means that we are expected to be self-sufficient apart from foodstuffs. Fortunately I do have some limited authority to make purchases on the local market, which would be in Deadwood.''

Longarm was struck by the fact that the officer seemed more conscious of his command's shortcomings regarding supply than he did about his military mission here. But then Longarm remembered that Wingate did say his expertise lay in the area of supply. Logistics, Wingate called it; plain old boring supply was what it actually was.

"If I remember correctly, that tall lodge with the red and black buffalo design is Tall Man's," Longarm said.

"Is it? I don't recall."

You damn well should, Longarm grumbled silently to himself. In case you have to lead a charge against these people.

Then it'll be too late to wonder where you should focus your attack.

But that was none of his business, really. And apparently was well beyond L. Thompson Wingate's command abilities too.

"Let's go see what Tall Man has to say. Then we'll ride on up the line an' meet Cloud Talker next." Longarm bumped his horse forward, and the supply officer—who seemed just about as completely out of his element here as a hog in a whorehouse—followed meekly along.

Tall Man grasped Longarm firmly by the upper arms in what was, for him, a warm embrace of welcome. "It has been too long, Longarm. You are well?"

"Yes. And you?"

"Two children since last we talked, but both girls." He made a face, then brightened and shrugged. "Next year a boy. I am sure of it."

"Yellow Flowers is carrying another child?" Longarm asked.

This time Tall Man grinned and puffed out his chest. "Not her, my friend. Yellow Flowers is a good woman and pretty, but she only gives me daughters. Now I have Yellow Flowers to prepare my food and keep my lodge but a new wife to make my sons." His grin got bigger. "Fourteen years old, this wife, and a belly soft as mouse fur. Big belly now." He laughed and held his hands in front of his own lean stomach as if cradling a cannonball. Or a kid. "A son. Yellow Flowers says so too."

"I'm happy for you, Tall Man. You should be proud."

"Yes, very."

"So tell me, Tall Man. What is the trouble here that you

would ask for me to come? You know I am always happy to visit with my friends the Crow, but it saddens me to think there may be a problem."

Tall Man looked at Wingate, then took Longarm by the elbow and pointedly turned his back on the officer, leading Longarm away in the direction of the grazing horse herd.

After a few paces he whistled to attract the attention of a boy of ten or eleven, then spoke rapidly in his own tongue. The boy nodded and raced away.

"Yellow Flowers will prepare a meal for our guests. It will be ready soon."

"You honor me."

"It is my pleasure to honor a friend who would come far without knowing why he comes."

"When you wish to tell me . . . ," Longarm suggested.

"Yes." They paced along in silence for several minutes, hiking up a hillside that overlooked the camp in one direction and the pastured horses in another.

"We are few," Tall Man said eventually.

"Yes."

"Outnumbered by the Piegan five, six to one."

"Yes." It was an exaggeration, of course. But what the hell.

"If we were many . . . ah, well. Those days are past. Sickness has taken many of our people away. Others have gone to live as if white, wearing shoes and trousers and working for wages in the far cities."

"Many?" Longarm asked.

"Too many. Our young people have become lazy. They do not want to rise up and fight the Piegan. Those of us who would fight are too few. And so we ask our friends to come and to speak for us against the lies of people who are not of our people."

"Lies, Tall Man? What lies?"

"These Piegan, you know how they lie."

Longarm nodded solemnly. It was true. The Piegan did lie. Damn near as much as the Crow.

"This time they say the Crow are murderers. They want to see a Crow hanged from a tree like a prairie chicken hung in the bush to age. They say if they do not have justice, they will break the pipe of friendship we gave to them when first we came here. They will break the pipe and they will kill all our people, even our children, and they will kill whatever of our women they do not want to use as their whores and their wood carriers."

"I see." Longarm handed Tall Man a cheroot, then struck a match to light his own smoke and Tall Man's.

"If they come, we will fight, Longarm. We will die, but we will fight. They will kill us all, but the Piegan will know that the Crow are warriors still."

"They would know," Longarm agreed.

"We spoke in council. It would be better for our children to live so that there may always be Crow on the earth. It may be otherwise. But we would have you speak with those people. Your voice is our voice, Longarm. We know you will not betray us the way the men at the agency did."

Longarm raised an eyebrow, but Tall Man either did not see or chose to pretend that he did not. "I see Yellow Flowers outside my lodge looking for us, Longarm. Come. See my new daughters and meet my new wife. We will talk more later."

Longarm grunted an acknowledgment and followed his friend back the way they had come. He had no idea where Captain Wingate had gotten to, but apparently the blueleg soldier was not invited to lunch. Later, Longarm figured. Time enough to look for him later.

Chapter 13

There was the sound of scuffling outside. Panting and grunting from great effort. Shuffle of feet and smack of flesh on flesh. Whatever it was, politeness dictated that Longarm ignore it. He tried, reaching into the stew pot for a chunk of pale, boiled meat that was probably, judging from the faintly sweetish flavor, young dog. It was good, actually, cooked together with yams and wild onions and some herbs and spices that he did not recognize but which tasted just fine in the combination Yellow Flowers had put together.

Outside, the grunts and now some muttering continued as at least two men and possibly more wrestled and strained.

"You honor me with a meal this fine," Longarm said, directing his words to Tall Man, but knowing Yellow Flowers understood English quite as thoroughly as did her husband and knowing the older wife would be flattered.

As for the younger wife . . . she was pure berries and cream. So fine there ought to be a law against screwing her on the grounds that such an act would contaminate an edible commodity. Tall Man obviously felt no such constraints, however, for the girl's belly was as round as her eyes. She was five, maybe six months along, Longarm figured.

It would be just one hell of a shame if Longarm let things get out of hand here and some Piegan warrior decided to grab the girl—Longarm never had gotten a name for her—and knock her brains out with a war club. Hell of a shame; hell of a waste. No, sir, he couldn't let that . . .

"Long Arm. Come out, Long Arm." The voice was immediately followed by a loud grunt, the moist sound of meat hitting the ground, and something on the order of a cough, which Longarm took to mean somebody had had the wind knocked out of him out there. "Long Arm. Come."

Longarm looked at Tall Man and motioned past the buffalo hide wall of the lodge. "Would you excuse me, friend?"

Tall Man nodded and rose first, thus giving his guest permission to leave.

Longarm sucked the last remnants of stew broth off his fingers and winked at Yellow Flowers, then ducked his head to pass through the low flap that served as doorway for the lodge. He felt Tall Man's presence close behind.

Outside he found two Crow warriors on the ground, one of them bleeding rather badly from a split lip, and a thick-bodied, swarthy Piegan in fringed leggings and breechclout standing over them.

"You are the one who is known as the Long Arm?" the Piegan asked.

"I am," Longarm admitted.

"I am Cloud Talker, son of John Jumps-the-Creek."

Which explained rather a lot. Including why a Piegan who

Longarm never heard of before might have asked for Longarm to be assigned to whatever was going on here.

Longarm smiled. "Your father is a good man and a good friend, Cloud Talker. I look forward to sharing a meal and tobacco with him. It has been too long. Is he well? Is he here?"

"He is here, Long Arm, but my father is not well. He was murdered." Cloud Talker's arm rose and he aimed his forefinger into the face of Tall Man. "My father was murdered by this man and his people."

Tall Man glowered but said nothing, although it was apparent that he was having difficulty keeping his emotions under rein.

"My father's spirit cries out for justice, Long Arm. My father asks the Great Father in Washing Town for justice." Cloud Talker dropped the accusing finger and looked into Longarm's eyes. "My father asks his friend of the Long Arm for justice. My father asks that this man and his killers die. An eye for an eye, the black robes tell us, is the white man's way. A death for a death. This is what my father asks of his friend now."

"Nobody dies without a trial, Cloud Talker. The Great Father's justice requires that."

Cloud Talker shrugged. "As you wish, Long Arm. Have the trial that you want. Then they die." He looked from Longarm back to Tall Man. "But know this, Long Arm. My father's murderers must die for what they did. In the manner of the Great Father if you will. If not that, then the Piegan nation will do what must be done, and all the Crow will be swept from this place so that our people may remain here in peace and harmony with all the spirits. You understand this that I say, Long Arm?"

"I believe that I do, Cloud Talker."

"Good. I have no more to say." Cloud Talker grunted contemptuously down at the pair of Crow guards by his feet, then turned and stalked silently away.

That, Longarm thought, was one impressive damned Indian.

And a dangerous one too. He was a keg of powder just waiting for somebody to light his fuse.

Any-damn-body.

Longarm turned back to his friend Tall Man. Funny, he thought, how it seemed to've slipped Tall Man's mind that John Jumps-the-Creek was dead. A body would think the Crow should have mentioned that little fact.

But then there was an awful lot that Longarm did not know about how Indians thought. He expected that was not apt to change to any appreciable degree either.

"Let's go back inside an' finish our meal, old friend," Longarm suggested.

Chapter 14

Longarm rubbed his groaning belly. He'd passed being full half an hour ago. Now he was miserable. But it was the sort of misery that a man just had to like. That Yellow Flowers really was a fine cook. Longarm's extravagant compliments hadn't stretched the truth hardly at all.

The two men stood outside Tall Man's lodge now, having a leisurely smoke. There was no sign of Cloud Talker nor of the Crow guards who had tried to keep him away. Someone else seemed to be missing also.

"Any idea where I can find Colonel Wingate, Tall Man? Or at least the horse I rode in on?"

"Dull Sword went to see Agent MacNall. He took your horse with him although my people would have seen to its care."

"Dull Sword?" Longarm asked.

Tall Man grinned and barked out a short, sharp little laugh. "It is the name we call him by."

"Prob'ly fits," Longarm commented.

"Yes, so we believe."

"Tell you what, old friend. Whyn't you point me toward this Agent MacNall. I expect I'd best fetch up with the colonel. Wouldn't hurt t' talk to MacNall either."

"It is too far for a man to walk in those frozen moccasins," Tall Man said, looking pointedly down at Longarm's calf-high boots. Apparently the boots, which were perfectly comfortable from where Longarm stood, appeared restrictive and heavy to the Indian's eye.

"You got a better idea?" Longarm asked.

"Yes. I do." Tall Man motioned to the nearest Crow and said something in a crackle of swift words. The young warrior nodded, pleased with being appointed to do something for this chieftain and his guest perhaps, and dashed off in the direction of the horse herd. When he returned he was leading a pair of heavily muscled ponies, one a tri-color pinto with a ring of white around its eyes and the other a bright chestnut with the short barrel and dished face that suggested Spanish barb breeding somewhere back along its bloodline.

"Choose one," Tall Man offered.

With no hesitation Longarm reached for the single rein that was tied loosely around the chestnut's lower jaw. No hesitation because everyone knew that a horse with the white showing around its eyes was no damn good. Tall Man wasn't going to put anything over on him that easily.

"You are sure you want this one?" Tall Man asked, confirming Longarm's suspicions. Longarm obviously had been expected to choose the flashier, taller, sleeker-bodied pinto over the tough and solid little barb.

"I'm sure." Longarm took a quick step to give himself some momentum and leaped onto the chestnut's back.

It had been a while since he'd ridden bareback, and he was plenty glad the chestnut stood steady for him while he shifted his butt and found a secure seat that did not trap his balls tight against the pony's backbone and turn them into mashed *cojones*.

Tall Man swung onto the pinto's back and seemed instantly to become a part of the animal. Longarm had no idea how anyone could make that look so . . . so natural and easy, dammit. Especially since Tall Man was a good head shorter than Longarm and the pinto at least two fingers taller than the chestnut.

Tall Man pointed. "You see there, Longarm? Beyond the creek. That rise? Two rocks and then one?"

"I see where you mean."

"The agency buildings are past that rise, just beyond the two rocks. I will race you there. Unless you are afraid to lose to Lo the Stinking Indian."

"Somebody been giving you trouble, old friend? Remember, I been downwind from you today. I didn't come across nothing that'd wrinkle my nose."

"Forgive me. I was rude to a man who has long been my friend."

"There's nothing to forgive."

"Then will you race with an old friend, my friend?"

"Hell, yes, what's your wager?"

"One twist of my tobacco against one handful of your cigars," Tall Man suggested.

"That sounds fair. But I'll be damned if I know what I'll do with your nasty tobacco when I already got these fine cheroots to smoke."

Tall Man grinned again. "First, my friend, you must win. Then it is time to think about the spoils."

"Whenever you say."

"You see the meadowlark behind the grass there?"

"I see it," Longarm said.

"When it flies. That is when we go," Tall Man said.

"Fair enough. I—"

The bird took wing, and Tall Man's pinto was two jumps gone before Longarm jabbed the chestnut with his heels and joined the race.

Joined the race? Not hardly.

The plain fact was, Longarm'd been jobbed.

Tall Man had seen his chance and climbed all over it.

That pinto could spot an antelope half a furlong and come in four lengths ahead, Longarm was sure.

Hell, he'd never seen a horse as quick as that pinto was. Seemed that way anyhow.

But jeez, wherever would an ignorant savage like old Lo there—if that's what Tall Man wanted to be called—learn about white men's aversion to horses with white eyes?

Wherever or however it had happened, Tall Man had taken advantage of it to make sure he was riding the pinto while Longarm plodded along—relatively speaking—on the chestnut.

The chestnut, meanwhile, was game and willing. It wasn't the horse's fault that nothing short of a runaway steam engine was apt to head that pinto. And only if the race went on until the pinto wore down.

Lordy, that horse could run.

Even so, Longarm was no quitter. And who knows? Maybe the pinto would have to stop to take a crap. Or Tall Man would decide to pause at the creek for a drink. Or . . . something.

Longarm yelled his throat raw trying to urge the chestnut

faster, and all the while the damned pinto was pulling an ever-widening lead on him.

They ran belly-down across the lush grass bordering the creek to crash full speed into the water.

The pinto's flying hoofs shot a curtain of water high into the air, the droplets glistening like jewels in the slanting afternoon light, and for a brief moment the angles of sun and vision lined up just right so that Longarm could see a miniature rainbow hanging over the creek behind the pinto's sweeping tail.

Tall Man was already back onto dry ground by the time Longarm and the chestnut plunged into the water. Longarm could feel the coolness in the air where the pinto had sprayed water before him, and the splashing of his chestnut soaked him past his knees.

He kept hoping the damn pinto would take a tumble. If the horse broke a leg, Longarm thought, it might yet come to a fair contest.

Not this time. The pinto disappeared over the rise and Tall Man with it.

Damned arrogant Indian wasn't even bothering to lean low over the pinto's withers at this point, Longarm noticed. Tall Man was riding bolt upright, turning back every few rods to taunt Longarm with laughs and short, choppy war whoops.

Helluva way to lose a handful of good smokes, Longarm thought.

But he was smiling. He'd been had fair and square, hadn't he? And he would happily have given Tall Man the cigars anyway.

Besides, this would give the two of them something to talk about for years to come. Not the race, dammit, but the way Tall Man got Longarm to cheat himself in the bet. Oh, that was something Tall Man would tell around the fires time and time again when the menfolk gathered to smoke and visit and swap lies late into the night. No question about it. Longarm would be the butt of many and many a Crow yarn from now on.

Longarm and his chestnut, the game and plodding little son of a bitch, scrambled over the crest of the rise and pounded down the other side.

Tall Man was still out front. Way the hell out front at this point. Shrieking and whooping and yelling for all he was worth.

Down below, maybe a hundred fifty yards distant, Longarm could see a collection of log and sod buildings, in the middle of which was planted a tall lodgepole with a U.S. flag attached to its peak.

There were some people wandering around among the buildings, most of them staring now at the sight of Tall Man and a white civilian charging straight toward them.

The people were . . . oh, Jesus! Longarm moaned.

The men down there were pointing. Shouting. Some scattered and ran for cover. Others dashed onto the porch of the biggest building, grabbing up some objects there and running back out into the yard to form a short line.

"No! No, goddammit!" Longarm shouted.

The men at the agency were forming into a firing line, Longarm saw. It was rifles they'd grabbed off the porch. Big old Springfields they looked like.

They must believe they were being attacked. Or that Longarm was chasing Tall Man. Or some stupid thing like . . .

"No, don't."

Tall Man looked back at Longarm's shouting, dammit, and did not see the danger ahead.

"Stop. Tall Man, stop!"

For a moment Tall Man looked puzzled. And then he laughed again and shook his head.

Jeez, Longarm thought. Tall Man thought Longarm was trying to trick him into losing the race. The stupid fucking race.

"No!"

Tall Man's head swiveled to the front again. And he saw.

He was within fifty, sixty yards of the line of men.

Half a dozen muskets were bearing on him.

Tall Man saw. Faltered. He yanked on the rein of the pinto and clamped his legs tight on its barrel, and the horse went into a butt-down slide in instant obedience to the command.

"Ready," Longarm heard from ahead. "Aim."

The pinto was sliding to a stop and Longarm's chestnut continued its headlong plunge down the slope.

Longarm jerked his rein to send the chestnut square into the line of fire.

As the chestnut thundered up behind the pinto Longarm dimly heard the command, "Fire!"

Longarm launched himself off the chestnut, slamming into Tall Man's back and sending them both tumbling while the air around them filled with the nasty, whipcrack sizzle of heavy musket balls slicing past.

Longarm felt a jarring, numbing impact on his right side. His vision clouded. But only for a moment. There was that moment of darkness.

And then there was nothing at all.

Chapter 15

"He's breathing." The words came from far away. Longarm wasn't really paying very much attention. It was just fine being where he was right now and doing what he was doing. Whatever that was. It was comfortable enough anyway. He felt like he was stretched out in a tub, or maybe it was a pool of lukewarm water, and that he was floating there. It was almost like floating on air except, of course, that was not possible, so he had to assume he was floating in water and just couldn't feel it because it was body-warm.

"I thought he was dead for sure."

"Just knocked out, I think."

"Anything broken?"

"Don't know." Longarm felt hands probing his ribs and chest and down around his back. One of the touching hands found a sore spot, and Longarm winced.

"He's coming around."

"I sure did think he was dead."

"Not yet." The hands poked and prodded and moved around on his torso. "If there's anything broken I can't find it this easily. We'll know for sure when he wakes up."

"What if he doesn't wake up?"

"Then he'll be dead, dammit, and we'll know something busted."

"Oh. Yeah."

Longarm's eyelids fluttered, and after another few moments opened.

He did not want to wake up. Not really. It had been nice and comfortable where he was before. Waking up hurt like hell.

"Colonel," he said, nodding.

Wingate was kneeling close by, a worried look pinching his mouth into a knot and putting deep furrows in his forehead.

Cloud Talker was standing several paces behind the infantry officer. There were some armed Piegan close around Cloud Talker, each of them carrying an ancient Springfield rifle with the post-war conversion to turn what originally was a muzzle-loading musket into an almost-as-useless .50–70-caliber breechloader.

There were also several white civilians Longarm had never seen before. Two of these were bent over Longarm and seemed to have been the ones conducting the examination.

Longarm's mouth was dry and he wanted a smoke. And a drink. And . . . A cold shiver ran up his spine as he remembered what had happened.

"Tall Man," he said. "Where's Tall Man."

"I am here." Tall Man had been standing near Longarm's head, out of his line of sight. Now the Crow came around beside Longarm's waist. "You saved my life, my brother."

"Question is," Longarm said, "was it worth it. I'd've won

73

our bet sure if I'd let these fellas shoot you outa the saddle."

Tall Man grinned. "You are not injured. I am sure of that now."

"Maybe. Might be I'll need some more o' Yellow Flowers' cooking to get me feelin' better."

"Then you shall have it," Tall Man promised.

"Cloud Talker," Longarm asked, "why'd your warriors try an' kill me just now?"

Cloud Talker scowled. "They try to shoot Tall Man. Not you, Long Arm."

"All right, dammit, why'd they go an' try to shoot Tall Man then?"

"These are agency police, Long Arm. Always try to stop trouble. They see Tall Man coming. Hear his war cries. See you chase him behind." Cloud Talker shrugged. "They grab their guns and try to help."

"Big help," Longarm groaned.

Cloud Talker's gaze shifted from Longarm to Tall Man. "If you do not spoil the shooting, no more trouble, eh?" Without another word he spun on his heels and stalked off, the squad of tribal police trailing in his wake.

"Nice fellas," Longarm muttered, then held a hand up so Tall Man could grab hold and help pull him to his feet.

Longarm looked at the white men who had been trying, however ineffectively, to doctor him. "My name's Long." He smiled. "I always try an' make an impressive entrance when I'm gonna meet somebody new."

A short, balding, friendly-looking fellow wearing a suit and clerical collar, a little detail Longarm hadn't noticed before, laughed in response. "In that case, sir, you most certainly accomplished your purpose. Allow me to introduce myself. I am the Reverend Ames MacNall. And you, of course, would

74

be the legendary deputy marshal known as the Long Arm of the law.''

"Just Longarm will do, Reverend.''

"Just Ames will do, Longarm.''

"Fair enough, sir.'' Longarm offered his hand, and the ruddy little preacher, who also happened to be the resident agent in charge of the Upper Belle Fourche Intertribal Agency, took and shook it.

MacNall introduced the other men still present. They were Charles Prandel, who was MacNall's assistant, Booth Watkins, agency procurement officer, and Cale Rogers, a teamster not attached to the agency.

"Are you all right now, Longarm?" MacNall inquired.

"I hurt like hell but I don't think anything's busted. Just lost my wind when I hit the ground. How 'bout you, Tall Man?''

"I am well. Thanks to you.''

"Yeah, well, you're lucky I didn't have time to think about that bet.''

"Tall Man tells me you were engaged in a horse race?" MacNall asked. His tone of voice suggested he thought surely Tall Man was lying about such a thing. Surely no grown man would engage in anything so frivolous.

"That's right. Seemed a good idea at the time.''

"Are you feeling well enough to ride?" Captain Wingate asked.

"Hell, I dunno. Haven't thought about it yet. Why?''

"It is getting late. And, um, Mr. Rogers tells me someone hired a wagon at Deadwood to carry passengers to Camp Beloit. I want to return to my command. There may be dispatches waiting there for me.''

Longarm felt of his ribs, then rubbed at his chin for a moment. "Colonel, I hurt from the ground up, an' I don't much feel like riding all the way back to Beloit. How's about I keep the borrow of that horse until tomorrow. I can find my way back when I need to."

"But where will you stay? Your equipment is all in a tent at the post."

"I'll bunk in with Tall Man an' his family." Longarm winked at his friend. "He owes me, you know. I intend to collect."

"You are perfectly welcome to stay here at the agency headquarters if you prefer," MacNall put in. "We have a room reserved for visitors. It isn't much, but it might be more agreeable than, um . . ." The reverend glanced toward Tall Man, obviously not wanting to put it into words, but probably convinced that no white man could remain alive and healthy after an overnight stay with savages.

"I'll be fine. Really. An' like I said. Tall Man owes me. I figure to let him wait on me hand an' foot this whole night long."

"Owe you? Do you forget already who it is that owes who? My cigars, brother. You lost the race so it is you that has the debt. Pay me."

"Or?"

Tall Man laughed. "Or it will be Burned Pot who cooks for you this night and not Yellow Flowers."

"That bad, huh?"

"Why do you think she was given such a name?"

Longarm chuckled and handed over the cheroots he owed Tall Man, reserving a couple for himself, however. "Tall Man, old friend, I want to talk to Reverend MacNall for a while. What say I join you at your lodge before time for supper."

"As you wish, Longarm." Tall Man left, and soon Captain Wingate did also.

"Did you want to speak with me in private?" MacNall asked.

"If it wouldn't be an imposition, yes, sir."

MacNall nodded a dismissal to his employees, and the teamster wandered off with them. "This way, sir. We may as well be comfortable while we talk."

Chapter 16

Comfortable for the reverend was mighty comfortable indeed, at least in Longarm's uninformed opinion. After all, what did he know about how the clergy were supposed to take their sacramental wine?

The Reverend Ames MacNall took his in the form of aged brandy, superb cigars, and service provided by a most comely little Piegan girl.

Not that there was anything wrong with any of that, Longarm conceded. As far as Longarm knew there wasn't a damn thing wrong with strong spirits taken in moderation, nor with a taste for quality in the innocent things that can give a man pleasure. As for the pretty girl, well, there seemed no reason why a man should have to hire an ugly female if he happened to need help around the place anyhow, not when a pretty one would do the same job just as well.

"Is there anything else I can do for you, Marshal?" MacNall asked.

"Reverend, I'm just about as content as a man can get right now. Well . . . pretty near to it, anyway."

MacNall smiled and nodded and, after glancing in the direction of the young Piegan servant, winked. "I believe I know what you mean, sir."

Which more or less proved, Longarm supposed, that preachers can be damn near human sometimes. "There is something I'd like to ask."

"Anything," the Indian agent said. "That is what we are here for, are we not?"

"Yes, sir. The thing is, I been noticing the way you talk and . . ."

"The accent? Ohio. I am from Ohio, Marshal."

"No, sir, that isn't it. It's that you aren't one to say thee an' thou an' all that stuff."

"Ah, you mean you thought I was a member of the Society of Friends? A Quaker, that is?"

"Well I just kinda, you know, assumed. . . ."

MacNall smiled. "Not all Bureau of Indian Affairs appointees are Quakers, Marshal. I, for instance, am ordained in the Fellowship of the Redeemer."

"I see."

"It is a small denomination. Very fundamental. Would you like instruction in our views, Marshal?"

"Uh, thanks, Reverend, but, um, I think I'd settle for a refill o' this liquor."

MacNall laughed and motioned to the girl, who quickly brought the crystal decanter and filled both gentlemen's glasses.

"Thank you, my dear," MacNall said in a fatherly tone of voice. The girl mumbled something and backed away to what seemed to be her post, off in a corner of the room. A room which Longarm found to be quite a contrast with the rough quarters at Camp Beloit. He asked about the difference between the two locations.

"Yes, of course. But then you see, the military encampment is only now being established. To keep order on the agency reservation and, if necessary, to preserve the peace internally or impose punishments in the event of a general uprising. As for this headquarters, the Department of the Interior acquired the site intact, very much as you see it now. It originally was what you Westerners call a ranch. Only one. Perhaps you can imagine so vast a tract of land falling under the control of one individual. I cannot. But then, of course, I am accustomed to Eastern ways, while you may be more familiar with the way things are done here in the frontier territories."

"Yes, sir." Longarm helped himself to another swallow of the brandy and to a pull on the cigar. One was as fine as the other.

"I do not have details of the purchase. Is that important to your investigation?"

"No, sir, I'm sure it isn't. I was just curious. Somethin' that is important, though, is how you read the situation between these two tribes. Would you mind filling me in?"

"Glad to." MacNall's story was largely a repeat of what Tall Man had already explained. The Piegan shaman John Jumps-the-Creek had been murdered by a person or persons as yet unknown. The Piegan were convinced that the Crow killed John Jumper as an act of deliberate, and malicious, provocation. Neither side wanted the government involved in investigating the death, but if there had to be interference from outside, then both agreed they wanted a man known to be friendly to them—Longarm—to handle it.

"Doesn't it seem dumb right on the surface of things for

the Crow to start something when they're outnumbered three or four to one?" Longarm asked.

"It might, except they probably know that the Piegan are locked in what we would call a struggle for political control within their own tribe," MacNall said.

"This is the first anybody's mentioned anything about that."

"Frankly, Marshal, I'm not surprised. Tall Man and the Crow would want to feign ignorance to make it seem they would have no motive to kill John Jumps-the-Creek. That is, they would want to present themselves that way if they were guilty. It is equally possible that they are innocent and may not in fact have any knowledge of the battles for control going on within the Piegan tribe.

"And the Piegan themselves, well, they say very little about their own politics. I only hear bits and pieces of it myself."

"John Jumper would have told me," Longarm said. "He was a good man. If his son is anything like the father was, then maybe I can get Cloud Talker off alone an' get him to open up to me."

"I wish you luck. Cloud Talker tells me as little as possible. And I have to take what little he does say with a hefty dose of salt. Frankly, I am never entirely sure when he, or for that matter any other Piegan, is telling me the truth."

"There is that," Longarm agreed, finishing off the brandy.

"More?"

"No, thanks, this is plenty. Look, Reverend, do you at least know who's in conflict in the Piegan nation and what it is that they want?"

"I know Cloud Talker is one of the principals," MacNall said, "and I know that one of the issues is whether the tribe will remain peacefully here or if they will break out and try to force a return to their homeland.''

"Back to the Marias?'' Longarm asked.

"There, or possibly they would be content to join the Blackfeet at their agency. The Piegan and Blackfeet have a kinship, I believe, but I am not clear on just what the relationship is.''

"It's enough generally to know that they're what we might call cousins an' not try and get any further into it than that. It doesn't make much sense to a white man anyhow,'' Longarm said. "But it's a genuine bond as far as they're concerned. You want to remember that too. Could you send 'em all back to the Blackfoot agency if you decided that'd be the best thing for everybody?''

"Of course not,'' MacNall said. "I have some limited authority here at this agency, but none at all when it comes to the larger picture. I doubt the gentlemen in charge of things back in Washington would even welcome suggestions from me on the subject if those ideas were not in line with the policies already established.'' MacNall spread his palms and smiled. "I am a very small fish, Marshal, in a rather muddy pond.''

"I know the feeling,'' Longarm agreed. "Oh, yeah. Something else.''

"Yes?''

"The tribal police. Are the Crow involved in that too?''

"Not at this time,'' MacNall said. "The Crow arrived here relatively recently and at a time of transition between the previous administration and my appointment. To date there are no Crow policemen. I have, of course, cautioned the Piegan officers to exercise restraint and a sense of brotherhood when dealing with their Crow brothers.''

"You do understand, I hope, that the Piegan an' the Crow

82

ain't real likely to think of each other as brothers," Longarm said.

"Marshal," MacNall chided him in return. "We are all brothers upon this earth. We are all God's children in equal measure."

"That may be so when you're lookin' at them from a pulpit, Reverend, but there's times when the man with the biggest war club is somewhat more equal than his poorer-equipped brother."

"I do not see it that way, Marshal. Not at all that way."

"Yes, sir. Whatever you say." Longarm stood and set his glass aside, reaching down to shake the agent's hand. "Thanks for the entertainment, Reverend, an' for the information. They both been a help."

"Any time, Marshal. I am at your disposal, sir."

Longarm nodded to the girl—damned nice-looking—and made his way out of the former ranch house, now headquarters for the Upper Belle Fourche Intertribal Agency.

Death and politics, Longarm reflected as he walked back toward the Crow camp. Hell of a combination, those two.

Chapter 17

It was damned difficult trying to get any sleep in Tall Man's lodge. Not that Longarm was uncomfortable exactly. The grass mattress and buffalo robe were plenty comfortable to lie on.

It was the noise that was so distracting. All that moist, meaty slap-slap-slap of flesh on flesh that was bothersome.

Longarm supposed it was something one would become used to, living with an entire family inside one small structure. But damn, it was impossible to keep from listening. And from getting horny.

The thing was, Tall Man was having himself a fine old time fucking his young wife Whatshername. It took Longarm a moment to call the girl's name to mind. It finally came to him. Burned Pot.

He had no way to know if the girl's name was as appropriate as Tall Man claimed, but by now there were several things about the pretty little wife that Longarm could attest to.

Like, for instance, Burned Pot was a squealer and a grunter when she was having fun under the robes.

Her pregnancy didn't seem to be putting any restraints on Tall Man or on Burned Pot. Tall Man had cuddled up behind her, pressing tight against her round little butt, so that they were lying close together like a pair of nested spoons. From that point, with everyone save Longarm sleeping naked anyhow, it was no great leap from a hug to a humping, and Tall Man had made that transition.

Quite a while ago, in fact. Longarm wished to hell the man would come and get it over with. But every time the two of them got to thrashing and yelping to a fare-thee-well, Tall Man would slow down or even come to a halt in the proceedings, obviously wanting to drag out the enjoyment of the moment as long as possible.

Which was just fine for him, dammit, but not so much fun from a spectator's point of view.

Eventually Longarm decided he was either going to have to move out of hearing or join in. And he kinda suspected Tall Man did not want male companionship right at this very moment. Better to get up and take a hike in the cool of the night than to lie there getting all worked up with his balls aching and no hope of any relief ahead.

Accordingly, Longarm slipped out from under his borrowed blanket, made sure he had his smokes, and stepped into his boots.

Tall Man and Burned Pot were still hard at it when Longarm ducked under the tent flap and emerged into the chill night air.

He took a few deep breaths and lighted a cheroot, then ambled off toward the edge of the Crow encampment and beyond.

• • •

Ghosts. Two of them. Longarm did not believe in ghosts. He damn well did not. But there a couple of them were. One tall and one small and both of them drifting silent as wraiths—well, why not; they were wraiths, right?—down along the low ridgeline where Longarm was seated on a boulder to finish his cigar.

But . . . ghosts?

A chill raced up Longarm's spine. That is . . . he knew better. Hell, yes, he did. But he couldn't help thinking. . . .

Pale, these ghosts. Pure white in the starlight. No moon to help out, just the thin hint of visibility sneaking down from a cloudless sky.

But . . . ghosts?

"Don't come no closer without you tell me who you are," he said more or less in the direction of the ghosts.

The smaller one increased speed and came closer anyway. Longarm shivered. Then felt foolish as hell when the "ghost" turned out to be nothing but a white dog.

The dog sniffed Longarm's hands, its breath hot on cold flesh, then flopped down at Longarm's feet with its tail curled tight around its butt. Dang thing seemed perfectly content there too.

"Who are you?" Longarm asked the bigger ghost, which he took now to be a smallish human form dressed in a flowing white garment.

"I am Angelica." The voice was very soft and melodious.

All right then. Not a ghost. An angel maybe?

She damn sure looked angelic once she got close enough that Longarm could see a little.

Angelica had black hair flowing down to her waist—a fact that likely contributed to the seemingly ethereal disembodiment, the ghost-shape that is, when seen from afar in the star-light—and a slim, lovely shape that was thinly disguised by the draped cloth of her pure white raiment.

Her face was small and her eyes large. From what Longarm could see, she was uncommonly pretty.

He guessed her age at nineteen or twenty, something in that general vicinity anyway.

She came over and sat on the flat rock close by his side as casually as if they'd been fast friends since childhood, never mind that his childhood was probably twice as far back in time as hers had been. Angelica seemed entirely at ease in the company of a stranger in the middle of the night.

"Are you, uh . . . I mean. . . ." Shit, he didn't know what-all he wanted to ask.

Angelica smiled. "You are Long Arm," she said. God, he could spend the rest of the night just sitting and listening to her voice. It was like hearing fine music for the first time.

"Yes," he agreed, that being about the only thing he could think of to say at the moment. There was something about this girl Angelica that had him as tongue-tied and nervous as a schoolboy at his first church social.

"Thank you for coming here. It is late, and I know you are tired. Forgive me for calling you."

Longarm frowned. Calling him? Damned if that was so.

Angelica smiled. Longarm felt something inside his chest spin around in circles, and there was a hollowness in his belly that he hadn't noticed before now.

"No," the girl said calmly, "you did not hear in your ears. Only in your heart." As if that explained something.

"You, uh . . ."

"Yes. It was I who called you here. I and this wolf who will help you when the spirits decide the time is come."

"Wolf," Longarm repeated slowly. He looked down beside his feet. There wasn't a wolf anywhere around. Just this big white dog. He wasn't sure what kind of a dog it was, except that it looked like the furry, heavily muscled dogs he'd seen up in the north country. The Canadians liked to use those dogs to haul sleds and sledges and such during winter. But those dogs were mostly dark-colored and smaller than this one. Otherwise this dog had the right shape and coat texture.

He reached down and the dog licked his hand, its tongue warm and wet, and he scratched behind its ears, then again at the base of its tail. It liked that just fine, pointing its muzzle high and wagging its tail while he scratched.

"Wolf," Longarm repeated.

"Yes," the girl said agreeably.

"Not a dog."

"No, Long Arm. A wolf. A spirit wolf."

"Uh, huh." Hell, he wasn't going to argue the point with her. It was commencing to look, though, like the girl was a tiny bit daft. Mighty fetching to look at. But her basket seemed to be a couple pecks shy of full.

Angelica laughed.

"Something funny?" he asked.

"You." She laughed again. It sounded something like little bitty silver bells tinkling. Or that was the impression he got. "You think I am touched by the spirits."

He didn't say anything.

"I am, of course. But not in the way you think," she said.

"How are you . . . touched?" He figured it would be safe enough to use her own word for it.

Angelica smiled and laid her fingertips gently on his wrist. "I have been given sight and knowledge of things that are not of this world and of some other things that are."

"And these things will help your tribe, I take it?" Longarm asked.

"If they would be of harm, Long Arm, I would turn my face from them and throw away the gifts the spirits have given to me."

"You could do that?"

"Yes, of course."

"And you called me here so's I can help you help your tribe or, uh, somethin' like that?"

"Yes. See? You do understand. Even though you do not know how you have come to understand this."

"It's confusing," he said.

"When you accept the truth of it, it will no longer confuse you," the girl told him.

The dog—wolf, if she preferred—lifted its head, its ears pricked, and bounded to its feet. It acted like it was straining to hear something far away to the north, something perhaps in the Piegan camp that lay in that direction.

The girl stood too. "We must go now, Long Arm."

"But I thought. . . ."

"It is enough," she said. "We have met. We will talk more at another time."

He looked at her and felt an almost overwhelming impulse to grab her and kiss her and press her onto the ground where he could take her with the scent of crushed grass and wildflowers surrounding them.

The girl gasped and shivered so violently he could see it. "No," she said quickly. "Not that."

"What?"

"Not . . . what you are thinking. You tempt me, Long Arm. Please do not . . . do the thing you wish."

"No," he said, embarrassed to've been caught at being so

randy. "Not without you wanting it to happen."

"But do you not see? That is what frightens me. I do want this to happen. And it must not. Not ever."

"I don't underst—"

The dog huffed, a sharp exhalation of breath that was not an audible bark but which caught the attention as if the slight sound had been as loud as a howl.

Without another word of good-bye or of explanation Angelica spun away, the diaphanous cloth of her robe swirling.

The dog bounded swiftly away to the north and the girl ran after it, her movement so light and smooth that the appearance was as if she floated, even though Longarm knew damn good and well that she was just running over the hills.

Once more the two, the dog and the girl, looked ghostly and pale in the starlight.

And once more a chill chased its tail up and down the length of Longarm's backbone while he watched them fade out of sight.

"Jesus," he muttered aloud as he stood and took a moment to compose himself before starting back down the hill toward Tall Man's lodge.

Lordy, but he did hope Tall Man and Burned Pot were done having at each other. He didn't think he could take much more in the way of temptation. Not all in one short night, he couldn't.

Chapter 18

Longarm shed his clothes—most of them anyway; he wasn't quite accustomed to this business of sleeping naked while others were close by and watching—and crawled under the blanket on the buffalo-robe bed he'd been given.

The interior of the lodge was warm and cozy after the cool of the outdoors, and Longarm was tired. Tall Man was snoring softly, and Burned Pot might have been asleep as well. For sure she had quit squealing, which Longarm found to be of considerable relief. He stretched, yawning, and wriggled around in search of comfort so he could doze off and . . .

His eyes snapped wide open.

He could feel something moving down by his waist. Sliding underneath the blanket. Finding flesh.

A hand. Someone was feeling around beneath Longarm's blanket.

Longarm blinked. Whoever it was wasn't content to just

feel. That someone was sliding into the bed with him now. But who . . .

"Longarm." The voice was a whisper, warm and faint in his ear. Yellow Flowers. He was sure of it. Pretty much had to be Yellow Flowers because as far as Longarm knew, she and Tall Man were the only ones in the lodge who spoke English. And it damn sure wasn't Tall Man who was climbing into bed with him.

"Yellow Flowers?"

Her response was a gentle kiss beneath his ear and an even more gentle squeeze of his cock.

"What are you . . . ?"

"Tall Man woke me when you left. He was ashamed. He enjoyed the body of Burned Pot and did not think of your needs. He told me to wait for your return and to make you comfortable."

"But . . ."

"It is all right, Longarm. Our ways are not all like yours. This that Tall Man gives is not wrong to us. It is but a way to make a friend and honored guest welcome and happy in our home. Allow me to pleasure you, Longarm. I am not so pretty as Burned Pot, but I am woman the same as she."

"Yellow Flowers, you're a fine an' beautiful woman. I mean that. But you don't have to . . ."

"Please, Longarm. Do not shame me by sending me away from your bed. Allow me to pleasure you in the way that a woman pleases a man."

He felt her hand caressing his cock and his balls, and his response was past his control even had he wanted to refuse. There was no way he could pretend disinterest now. Not with what Yellow Flowers was holding onto.

Besides, dammit . . . he didn't want to shame the wife of a

generous friend. That wouldn't hardly be polite, now would it.

Yellow Flowers dipped her head and began to lick Long-arm's right nipple. The sensation of it tingled all the way down into his groin, and he commenced to moan and squirm on the coarse, matted hairs of the buffalo robe.

Her fingers continued to toy with and tickle his balls while she licked and suckled first one nipple and then the other. Longarm's breath began to come faster and hotter.

Yellow Flowers took her time about her ministrations to him. Not that she needed more time to get him aroused and ready. Practically from the first touch he was hard as an all-day sucker, and after a couple minutes he thought he was sure to burst apart at any moment, just purely explode like a Chinese popper on the Fourth of July.

He reached for her, finding her skin soft and smooth and cool to the touch. He cupped her breast, then slid his hand down to her ass, which was nicely shaped and firm with muscle. He squeezed one cheek and tugged, pulling her on top of him.

Yellow Flowers continued to lick his left nipple while she straddled his hips and lowered herself onto Longarm's waiting shaft.

She guided his spear into her body with one hand and tweaked his right nipple with the other.

Yellow Flowers was wet and receptive. Her pussy was surprisingly tight considering that she'd borne two daughters to Tall Man. She gasped a little when she felt the size of the tool that entered and filled her, but if she felt any pain or discomfort she did not show it. If anything she appeared to relish this massive intrusion into the most private recesses of her body.

She took him deep into herself and remained poised there

for long moments, as if memorizing the exquisite feeling.

Then, slowly at first, she began the rhythmic rise and fall of the ageless dance that joins man and woman.

Her hips pumped and churned, and Longarm's responses were quick and powerful.

He had been primed once by the noises Tall Man and Burned Pot had made. Teased anew by the compelling presence of the ghost girl Angelica. And now given respite by Tall Man's generosity and Yellow Flowers' willing body.

Long before he wanted this to end Longarm felt his juices gather in his balls like boiling water being pumped forcefully into a rubber bladder.

The pressures rose, higher and ever higher, until he could no longer contain them.

With an involuntary groan of deep satisfaction Longarm felt the inevitable explosion.

Wave after diminishing wave of hot fluid spurted out of him, washing Yellow Flowers' hole and spilling back out again to flow onto his balls in a hot and sticky flood of semen.

Yellow Flowers sighed, seeming quite pleased herself, although he did not think she had reached a climax of her own, and kissed first one of his nipples and then the other before she raised herself from him and allowed his prick to slide free of her warmth into the cool of the air.

"Wait," she whispered. "I will wash you. Then you can sleep."

He felt her leave the bed. Moments later she was back, this time with a wet, slightly warm cloth that she used to wipe his cock and his balls.

Longarm sighed. He never felt Yellow Flowers leave his bed the second time.

He was deeply contented now, and was asleep before she had time to finish cleaning him.

Chapter 19

Longarm gnawed the prairie hen leg bone to a high polish, then tossed it out of the lodge—the skirting down along the ground had been rolled up to let some air circulate—to where a pack of brown and black dogs were waiting to quarrel over the scraps.

All the dogs that he could see, around this lodge and gathered close by all the others in sight, were browns and blacks and spotted combinations of those two main colors. There wasn't a solid-white dog anywhere within his range of vision. Longarm couldn't help but wonder if Angelica was out traipsing over the hills with her white "spirit wolf" somewhere. The truth was that he wanted to see her again. She'd said they would talk more. But there were things other than conversation that interested him about the girl. She'd had—still did have—an enormously powerful impact on him. Damn unusual, that. He couldn't quit thinking about her. Not even after Tall Man's generosity with Yellow Flowers during the night. It was still

Angelica that he thought about and Angelica who stirred his loins whenever he did bring her back to mind.

"About last night . . ." Longarm said, offering his friend a smoke and bending forward to pluck a grass stem and set it aflame in the cooking fire that burned low in the center of the lodge.

"It was nothing," Tall Man insisted, biting the twist off his cheroot and spitting it toward the fire. He missed, the bit of dark tobacco falling instead into the meat pot, where it was allowed to remain, presumably as additional flavoring. "Do not mention it again."

Longarm nodded. And kept his mouth shut, that being how Tall Man wanted it done. After all, it was Tall Man's wife that Longarm had been given to use, and Tall Man was entitled to set the rules when it came to thanks . . . or to repeat performances.

"What do you plan today, my friend?" Tall Man asked. "Will you stay with us longer? You know you are welcome in my lodge."

"I know that and I thank you," Longarm said, grateful to be back on neutral ground when it came to this conversation. "But I dunno if I'll stay here a spell longer or go back to the army camp. I want to have another talk with Cloud Talker, of course."

"Yes. You need to speak with him when no Crow are present. And when the white agent and his spies cannot overhear."

"Spies?"

Tall Man shrugged and took up a wisp of dry grass to light his cheroot.

"I'll prob'ly come back here this afternoon anyhow," Longarm said. "I kinda want to talk with Angelica again."

"Angelica?" Tall Man asked. "Who is this person?"

"You know. Angelica. Pretty girl. Has a big white dog. Hell, Tall Man, she's one of your people. I figured you'd know where I can find her."

Tall Man frowned. "But Longarm, my friend. I do know all of my people. And there is no Crow woman named Angelica and none who has a large white dog, no."

Longarm was frowning too now. And was becoming damned well confused.

Chapter 20

Longarm entered the Piegan camp from the south, mounted on the horse he'd borrowed from Colonel Wingate's subordinate back at Camp Beloit. Tall Man had offered him the use of that slow-footed chestnut again. And then liked to burst a gut laughing at how he'd gulled his old friend into losing a race. But then Longarm could expect the teasing to be repeated over and over again for as long as he knew Tall Man. Which meant for as long as the two of them lived. Sneaky damned Indian!

He rode among the Piegan lodges now, and recognized several of the tribal police he'd seen the day before. The difference was that today none of them was shooting at him, although they all had their long, clumsy old .50–70 Springfields either in hand or mighty close by. Apparently, though the converted muskets kicked like so many mules and had accuracy on the order of a pebble being thrown with a slingshot—except maybe not quite that accurate—the old ballbusters were a badge of honor among the native police. Every one of them that Longarm saw had been burnished to a high gloss, wood and metal alike. With that kind of caring for, rare among Indians, the old guns looked as good as new. Which wasn't all that good to begin with, of course, but what the hell. Even these old trapdoor conversions were better than a bow or a war club when it came to serious scrapping. And if a man ever did get close enough, or lucky enough, to put a ball into his target, that sonuvabitch was damn sure down and out. The guns threw a bullet roughly the same size and shape as a grown man's thumb, and when they hit it was no delicate little wound. It was more on the order of having a hod full of bricks drop onto the poor soul on the receiving end of the deal. All in all, Longarm was just as glad that he hadn't been hit yesterday.

Today, however, the tribal police seemed cordial enough. At least to the point of not shooting at him. Longarm reined straight at a dark-complected Piegan with scars on his cheeks that were too symmetrical to have been inflicted by accident.

"I'm looking for Cloud Talker."

The Piegan scowled and shook his head, pointing to one ear as if to indicate he either couldn't hear or couldn't understand.

"You understood English just fine yesterday. Heard just fine too," Longarm told him. Not that Longarm had paid any attention to the Piegan at all the day before. It was a shot in the dark, but one he figured couldn't do any harm. Hell, if the guy really couldn't speak the language, then none of this was making any sense to him anyhow and the bluff would pass unnoticed.

"That lodge," the policeman said, pointing.

"Thank you very much." Using the spur on the side of his

horse that the Piegan couldn't see, Longarm gigged his horse sharply in the ribs, causing the animal to jump as if skittish. It "accidentally" bumped into the policeman and caused the sullen Piegan a small loss of face by making him scurry to get out of the way. "Sorry." Longarm made a show of bringing the horse back under control, then put it into a trot toward a squat, wide-based lodge that was decorated with zigzag lightning bolts, sun shapes, and bright red chevrons.

He brought the horse to a halt before the lodge door and called out, "I have come to talk with the son of my friend."

After a moment the door flap was thrown open and Cloud Talker stepped outside, followed by two very handsome young women who Longarm took to be Cloud Talker's wives. If there were children, they remained out of sight in the lodge.

"Welcome, Long Arm. Get down. Let my woman take your horse." He said something over his shoulder, and the younger of the women came forward to take the reins from Longarm and lead the horse away. Cloud Talker said something else, and the older woman bobbed her head and went into the lodge. She returned moments later carrying a pair of mats, which she unrolled beside a now-cold ash pit where at night the men could sit in comfort to talk and scratch.

Longarm found it interesting that Cloud Talker did not invite him inside the lodge for meat and serious hospitality. Still, Cloud Talker only knew Longarm by reputation. It was John Jumps-the-Creek who had been Longarm's friend.

Thinking about the old man, Longarm wondered what had happened to his wives. Longarm had liked them, the one known as Juanita Maria in particular. Longarm had given her a comb of honey once, and the toothless old thing had fawned over him ever afterward.

"Where are your father's wives?" Longarm asked without thinking as the two men settled onto the mats.

Cloud Talker frowned, then said, "My father's wives went back to their families, as is right and proper."

"That's good," Longarm said. "Before I leave the agency I would like to see them again and bring them presents. They were kind to me when your father was alive." He didn't bring up the fact that it was most definitely *not* a right or proper thing for Cloud Talker to turn the old women out of his lodge after his father's death. But then, obviously Longarm wasn't supposed to know that.

"I will see that my father's wives receive whatever you would give to them," Cloud Talker said. Which, of course, was not at all what Longarm had offered. Curious, Longarm thought. Damned curious.

"Thank you for receiving me today," Longarm said. He pulled out a twist of tobacco he'd gotten from the agency sutler on his way over and handed it to Cloud Talker. "Will you smoke with me?"

"Yes, Long Arm." Cloud Talker said something to his wife, and she went into the lodge for a pipe and burning glass, which she presented to her husband. Cloud Talker drew his knife and shaved tobacco into the pipe, tamped it lightly with the ball of his thumb, and lighted it using the magnifying glass. He smoked in silence for several moments, then handed the pipe to Longarm.

Longarm adopted a solemn and serious mien as well, and sat cross-legged and silent for long minutes while he smoked and contemplated. Or pretended to. If Cloud Talker wanted seriousness, then seriousness the Piegan leader would jolly well get.

Eventually Longarm grunted, signifying absolutely nothing, and returned the pipe to Cloud Talker.

Cloud Talker sent puffs of smoke to the four ends of the earth, then said something in a low, singsong chant and carefully laid the pipe aside. "What is it my father's friend Long Arm would seek from me?" he asked.

"Information," Longarm said. "If I'm gonna find out who it was that killed my friend, I must first know how he died."

"The Crow murdered my father," Cloud Talker said.

"Yes, so you say. But I have to determine that on the record so the agency and the Crow will believe it too."

"The Crow," Cloud Talker repeated. "They are the ones who murdered my father."

"Which particular Crow do you think did it, Cloud Talker? Tall Man? Some other? Tell me what you believe to be true."

"Does it matter which Crow struck the blow? The Crow are no good. None of them. They should not have been brought to this that is our land. They should be sent away, Long Arm. They are all guilty."

"But who is it should hang for the murder, Cloud Talker?"

"Does it matter?"

"Yes, Cloud Talker. It does."

"They are all guilty. Send them away. Leave us in peace while still there is peace to keep, Long Arm. Tell the Great Father this. Tell him to send the Crow from our land and there will be peace. If the Crow remain"—Cloud Talker shook his head—"I see war between our peoples. Tell this to the Great Father, Long Arm. Tell him there must be war if the Crow do not pay for the death of my father."

"Tell me about the death of your father, Cloud Talker. Tell me about the murder of this man who was my friend."

"I have said what I wish to say to you, Long Arm. I welcomed you as a friend and I gave you the pipe to smoke. Now go. Tell the Great Father what I, Cloud Talker, shaman and chief of the Piegan, said to you. Tell him all this that I have said.'' Cloud Talker made a chopping motion with his right hand, then abruptly stood and strode off away from Longarm and his own lodge.

''Shit,'' Longarm mumbled. But there wasn't any point in chasing after Cloud Talker. The man had said all he was likely to. This time, anyhow. Longarm stood too, reaching into his pocket for a cheroot. Dammit anyhow, he thought.

Chapter 21

The horse had been staked out on a patch of sparse grass behind Cloud Talker's lodge. Longarm flipped his near stirrup onto the seat of the saddle and reached for the latigo, intending to tighten the cinch and head back to the Crow camp. He paused before pulling it snug, however.

He was already among the Piegans, and still had tied behind his cantle the rest of the presents he'd expected to give to Cloud Talker. Before, that is, the Blood shaman had stalked off in a huff.

In addition to the twist of tobacco that he'd given to Cloud Talker, Longarm had earlier bought and brought along two more twists of molasses-soaked tobacco and one pint of sugar and another of coffee.

It seemed a shame to haul those around when they could serve to bring some smiles to the old women who once were married to John Jumps-the-Creek. And hell, Longarm was here now and had some time to spare. He might just as well look up Juanita Maria and . . . what was the other wife's name? Teeth, tooth, something about teeth. Of course. Bad Tooth. But then, as he remembered it, Bad Tooth at least had some teeth left in her head to *be* bad. Juanita Maria didn't.

With thoughts such as those in mind, Longarm dropped the stirrup back onto its leathers without tightening his cinch, and instead untied the burlap sack the agency sutler gave him to hold his purchases.

He stopped at Cloud Talker's lodge and asked the young wife there, "Where can I find the wives of Cloud Talker's father?"

The girl shook her head, but the other wife came up behind her and addressed Longarm over the younger wife's shoulder. "At the far north edge of the camp there is a lodge, very old, with three buffalo on it. That is the place of the son of Bad Tooth's sister. That is where the woman called Bad Tooth lives."

"Thanks." Longarm touched the brim of his Stetson and hiked off to the north.

Ten minutes later he decided he should have gotten the horse off its tether. He didn't mind a little walk. But this Piegan camp was two, maybe three times the size he'd expected to find.

What had Wingate said about the number of Piegan warriors? Nine hundred or so? Damned if that was so. Longarm was no great shakes at estimating numbers, especially when it came to Indian camps, where one warrior might live in a single lodge or there might be a dozen bunking in that same amount of space. There were some experts who used a rule of thumb calling for there to be five warriors for every lodge in a given village. Whatever the case, Longarm was certain that the figure given to Wingate was way low. Maybe by as much as half the true strength of the tribe. Hell, there could be as many as two thousand fighting men available to the Piegan. And Wingate, with no field experience to draw on, had no way to so much as guess that he was being fooled.

One thing Longarm was sure of. If hostilities broke out between the Piegan and the Crow, there wouldn't be a Crow of any shape or age alive longer than an hour or so. Tall Man's much smaller band would be wiped out in no time.

And considering how few blueleg soldiers Wingate had under his command at Camp Beloit, the same could easily happen to them with the second wave of screaming, blood-hungry Piegan.

The Piegan camp was strung out for well over a mile along a narrow creek run.

Longarm was sobered and thoughtful as he walked on and on among the Piegan lodges.

"Grandmother," Longarm said by way of greeting.

The old woman turned, her eyes growing wide and round as she saw who the visitor was.

She let out a shriek as if she'd been attacked by a grizzly bear, and began to yammer and scream in her own language, at which the younger women who were nearby commenced to buzz and mutter amongst themselves. Longarm had to wonder just what line of bull old Bad Tooth was giving them. Powerful stuff, he suspected, based on the way eyes rolled and expressions dashed from joy to horror and back again.

It was probably just as well that he didn't understand a word of it, he thought, because if he did he might feel compelled to correct some of the more glaring fabrications. And what can ruin a good yarn quicker than the truth, eh?

Bad Tooth jabbered at the other women for a while, then

jumped up from the pegged-down coyote skin she'd been scraping and ran—well, hopped and hobbled in something approximating a run—into another lodge close by. She emerged from it moments later with Juanita Maria, every bit as excited as Bad Tooth, hard on her heels.

Longarm smiled. He'd found the both of them, and neither woman looked like she'd changed the least bit since last he'd seen them.

Of course the last time he'd spoken with these two old crones, they'd had the security and respectability of marriage to their tribe's leading citizen.

Now, with John Jumps-the-Creek dead, they were burdens on their relatives. Hangers-on who could hope for a few scraps and leftovers at best, and who might well starve to death if the man who sheltered them ran short of food come the next winter. The life of an aging widow in most tribes that Longarm knew of was precarious under the most favorable of circumstances, and impossible—quite literally so—when things were not going well. An unproductive old person, man or woman, was apt to be turned out into the snow with neither blanket nor food as a means of preserving the food supply for those who were younger and stronger and able to pull their own weight in the daily routines.

Today, though, these two particular old women were alive.

And seemed extremely happy to receive this visit from a friend.

Longarm, Bad Tooth, and Juanita Maria were all grinning when they ran to him and began hugging him with all their wiry strength.

Chapter 22

"Here. No, the sugar is for you, Juanita Maria; I know how much you like your sweets. No, Grandmother. All of it. I brought it only for you."

Juanita Maria spoke no English, so Bad Tooth translated for her. Juanita Maria, who had been the wife of John Jumps-the-Creek's youth, was crying by the time Bad Tooth was done talking. Either Juanita Maria was becoming mighty sentimental in her old age, or Bad Tooth was gilding the lily somewhat in her speachifying. Either way, both women seemed happy, and that was what counted. Longarm was glad he'd had time to come find them, gladder still that he could bring them a few small items to show that he still cared about them.

"How have you been?" he asked. "Are you well? Do they treat you with the respect and the kindness my grandmothers deserve?"

Juanita Maria said something in a sad and shaky voice, but Bad Tooth only shrugged by way of interpretation. "We have food to eat and robes to sleep on. It is enough," the old crone said.

"And Cloud Talker? Does he provide for you too?"

Bad Tooth shrugged again.

"May I ask you something, Grandmother?"

"Long Arm is welcome to say or to ask whatever he likes. Surely our grandson knows this."

"I can't seem to recall ever meeting Cloud Talker before. Which one of you is his mother?"

"Why, Cloud Talker is not of our blood, no. Not of either of us."

"But if John Jumps-the-Creek is his father . . . excuse me. I don't mean to bring up something that I shouldn't."

Bad Tooth translated that for Juanita Maria, and both of them seemed to get quite a kick out of the idea. "Long Arm, have you forgotten so very much about our people that you would ask such a thing? Cloud Talker is the son of John Jumps-the-Creek's sister Many Willows, whose husband was not of the same clan and so could not be the father to Cloud Talker."

Longarm frowned, trying to put it in place. He vaguely remembered that Piegan couples had to come from two separate clans in order to avoid the contamination of incest. There was a kinship within the clan regardless of blood connection. And when it came to family, whether clan or blood relationship, the children followed the line of the mother, not the father. That had something—Longarm had never really understood all this—to do with the habit of having an uncle act as father to the children of his sister. In many tribes a blood father's relationship with his own children was minimal, almost to the point of disappearing.

He really didn't understand all of the complex interlock of

family and clan relationships. But at least the reminder was enough to satisfy his curiosity about Cloud Talker. And to explain the fact that Longarm had never met him before even though Longarm and John Jumps-the-Creek had been friends for years.

"Is that . . . Cloud Talker being, uh, sort of a son to my friend . . . is that why Cloud Talker is the new shaman?"

"Cloud Talker our shaman? Is he?" Bad Tooth asked, her rheumy old eyes growing wide.

"But I thought. . . ."

Bad Tooth and Juanita Maria conferred; then they led Longarm to the fire pit outside the lodge where Juanita Maria stayed. "Sit. We will talk for a while, before the rain begins again."

Longarm looked at the sky. There were a few puffy clouds building to the west, but they presented no threat. The sky directly overhead was all buttermilk and blue. He doubted it would rain again all week long judging from the look of things at the moment. He did not presume to correct the old women, though. That would have been rude.

"Would you like coffee to drink?" Bad Tooth asked. "I can make some from the present you gave to me." A moment later, after some quick translating, she added, "Juanita Maria would sweeten your coffee with the sugar you brought."

"No, thanks. Those things are for you, not for you to serve me with."

"You would like water to drink?"

"I would like water, yes." He wanted them to be able to do something for him. That would demonstrate their hospitality. And their usefulness. He suspected both were of importance to the women.

Juanita Maria hurried away to fetch a gourd of cool water

110

for him, and Bad Tooth disappeared long enough to find a walnut-sized chunk of pemmican for their guest. Longarm saw the pemmican and felt his stomach churn. When properly made, pemmican would last for years without spoiling. Which seemed a helluva shame. The stuff, made of pulverized berries mixed with tallow and other ingredients best left unknown, looked and tasted like goat shit allowed to turn rancid. Well, tasted like he imagined rancid goat shit would taste. Except maybe not quite that good.

He accepted the pemmican, smiled broadly, and bit off a mouthful. Yeah, it was properly made pemmican, all right. Wonderful stuff.

A sip of the water wouldn't wash the taste away. He thought about munching a handful of dirt, or possibly some horse apples, but that would have been rude. He settled for finishing off the pemmican quickly so as not to have to endure it any longer than necessary and then lighting a cheroot to cover the flavor with something infinitely better.

Juanita Maria and Bad Tooth graciously accepted his last cheroot—he'd thought he had more than enough when he left Deadwood, dammit, but with the race yesterday and now this—and broke it in two pieces so they could share the slender cigar. Longarm held a match for them and lighted his own. "May I ask you something?"

"Long Arm can ask anything. Are we not the grandmothers of this good friend?"

"You are," he agreed, solemnly puffing on his cheroot and sending a wreath of pale smoke into a quickening breeze. "If it would not be too painful, Grandmother, please tell me how my friend died."

"Our husband was murdered by the Crow. The Crow are not to be trusted, you know."

"Yes, but do you know which man of the Crow murdered John Jumps-the-Creek?"

Bad Tooth and Juanita Maria conferred again. Then Bad Tooth shook her head. "It was night. Very late. We were asleep in our beds. I heard my husband stir. I saw him rise from his bed. He was growing old, Long Arm. He had to rise several times each night to go out and empty his bladder. You know how this is."

Longarm nodded.

"I saw him rise. No one called to him. No one woke him in the night. I am sure of this, Long Arm. Juanita Maria has no more hearing than she has teeth, but my ears are as good now as when I was a girl. If someone called to my husband in the night, I would have heard it as well. He woke with the need to piss as he always did, and he got up and he went outside into the night. I saw him go. He put a blanket over his shoulders and he went out of our lodge." She sighed, the memories seeming to overtake her for a moment, and paused to bring Juanita Maria up to date on what was being said.

"My husband stepped outside and spoke to someone. A greeting. I could hear but not well. He did not speak a name. Only the greeting. He knew this person. I heard no answer. A moment more I heard my husband's water splash. He was an old man and no longer had a strong stream when he pissed. When he was young he could piss with the force of a bull buffalo. This night I heard the splash of his piss on the ground soft and long. And then there was another sound. Like that of an unripe melon in July being broken on a flat stone. You know the sound I mean?"

Longarm nodded again.

"I heard my husband fall. His water was not splashing no more. Never more. He fell. I heard him. He did not cry out, did not moan. The Crow intruder killed him with a war club. Dashed his brains out like those of a puppy killed for the pot. My husband fell to the ground in the mud of his own piss, and the Crow killer went away.''

''Did you hear this, um, Crow killer leave?''

''You mean did he run away so that I could hear his footsteps? No. I heard only what I told to you already.''

''And you didn't see who it was that killed my friend John Jumps-the-Creek?''

''I did not have to see the killer, Long Arm. My husband knew only one man among the Crow. Only one who could have come so near to him in the night. That one is the one they call Tall Man, who is the leader of their vile people.''

''I see,'' Longarm said. ''But you didn't actually see. . . ,''

''I did not.''

Longarm thought about that for a time. He sighed. Dammit, a man is not given so many friends in his lifetime that he can afford to lose any. And now he had already lost one, and there was a strong possibility he might well lose another. First John Jumps-the-Creek. Perhaps Tall Man next. Both thoughts were lousy ones.

''Thank you for your help, Grandmother.''

''There is no need for thanks between us. You would do whatever I ask of you, as I will do whatever you need of me. That is the way it has always been between us.''

''Yes,'' Longarm agreed. ''So it has. Before I forget, Grandmother . . .''

''Yes?''

''A little while ago, when I mentioned Cloud Talker, you thought it amusing that I would call him shaman of your great people. But Cloud Talker himself claims to be shaman here. Is this not so, Grandmother?''

113

"Cloud Talker speaks of himself as shaman, that is so. There is another, more powerful, who would be shaman. And others still who would ask the people to follow them as leaders at council and in times of war. Not all the people look to Cloud Talker to lead them. Not in council, not even as shaman."

Politics, Longarm thought. It's everywhere, even in a Piegan camp in the middle of nowhere. He swallowed the last of the water he'd been given and stood, smiling. When he went to say his good-byes, though, Bad Tooth held up a hand in restraint as she listened to something Juanita Maria was telling her.

"Yes," she said. "Juanita Maria reminds me. I told you how my husband was killed. What I said to you was true. It is also true that it was Juanita Maria who found his body and not I. I went back to sleep after I heard the things I heard. You must understand that I did not know at the time what the noises meant. I thought only that my husband walked off to talk to whoever it was he saw in the night. It was later, no one knows how long, that Juanita Maria got up and went outside. Her bladder is weak with age too, you see. She went outside to piss, and it was she who found our husband lying dead on the ground with the dogs standing watch over his body. It was she who began the death chant that woke the rest of us. But Juanita Maria did not see the killer either. Our husband's body was cold and growing stiff by the time she found him. Is all this of help to you, Long Arm?"

"You've both been wonderful, Bad Tooth, Juanita Maria. You are very much of help to me. I hope I will have time later to visit with you again, Grandmothers. I have always enjoyed your kindness."

"You are always welcome, Long Arm, in our hearts as well as our lodges."

"Thank you."

"Hurry now or you will be wet."

He looked to the sky again. The clouds to the west were taller now and much closer, but he was sure it would not rain again. Certainly not today. He said his good-byes and started hiking south again toward Cloud Talker's lodge and the horse Longarm had left there.

Chapter 23

Longarm hunched his shoulders and gritted his teeth. He was pissed off. He was unhappy. Mostly he was soaked through to the skin.

The borrowed horse and its borrowed saddle did not have a slicker attached, and so he was riding now in a gray torrent of vicious rain and had nothing but the brim of his hat to ward off the barrels of rain that were being dumped on him every step of the way.

The rain had come up out of nowhere, sweeping across the prairie like an immense dark wall, lifting dust where the first icy drops struck dry soil and pushing that sharp, peculiar, ozone rain-scent ahead of it.

Now, minutes later, Longarm felt like he'd been thrown into a creek with all his clothes on. He would not have been any wetter if so. Could not have been.

And to make matters worse, the horse did not like the rain any better than Longarm did. It was becoming nervous, dancing and jumping and getting increasingly spooked. He had to ride on a tight rein and worry that the stupid creature might take a tumble as the muddy footing became more and more slippery.

Off to his left he could see the cluster of buildings that were the agency headquarters. A quartet of tribal police were gathered at the base of the flagpole trying to untangle the halyard there so they could get the flag out of the weather, and he could see some others enjoying the protection of the porch overhang, no doubt stationed there in comfort so they could offer encouragement and advice to those who were by the flagpole in the downpour.

The best thing, Longarm decided, would be for him to join those fellows on the porch. The ride back to Beloit could wait a spell longer.

Besides, those men with the tangled halyard very likely needed the exact advice he could give them.

He turned the horse away from its original line of travel and pointed it east instead. The horse, perhaps understanding, volunteered a rocking-chair lope to get out of the rain.

"I'm sorry, Marshal, but I don't have anything here that you'd like. You want another twist of cheap tobacco like you bought off me this morning, I got it. You want some sugar or coffee or tea, that's fine. Blankets I got, or knives or iron pots or the usual Indian trade geegaws. But fine cheroots? For that you gotta go to Deadwood or Cheyenne or someplace like that."

"What *do* you have?"

"To smoke? Cheap and nasty, Marshal, that's what I got. Two choices, really. I got these dark rum crooks. Lots of those. They taste like shit, but they come three for a nickel. And I tell you what. You being a white man of some discrimination,

I'll sell you my crooks four for a nickel. All you want of them.''

"You said there's another choice?''

The agency sutler grinned. ''Over there in the corner, Marshal, I got an old catch rope that some Injun gave me in a trade. That old rope has been drug through the manure and the dirt of God only knows how many corral floors and branding chutes. It's frayed and filthy and full of cow shit. But there's a good twenty, maybe twenty-two feet of it left in the coil. If you want, Marshal, I'll sell you that, the whole of it, for twenty-five cents. Whenever you want a smoke you just chop six inches or so off that rope an' light up. It won't taste much different from these crooks and will cost a hell of a lot less.''

Longarm couldn't help but laugh with him. ''Reckon I'll take some of those rum crooks, friend.'' He looked outside, where the rain continued to pound hell out of the ground with no sign it would let up inside a week's time. ''And I think I'll be needing some more gift stuff. Tobacco, sugar, like that. Couple dollars' worth of it, whatever you think would be good.''

With rain like this and miles between the agency and the army post, there was no way Longarm intended to get back on that horse. Not for any ride longer than the one that would take him back to the Crow camp.

It looked like Tall Man and his family would have an overnight guest again tonight.

Chapter 24

"The reverend is having devotions now, him and some of his friends."

Longarm thanked the civilian orderly and glanced outside. The rain was, if anything, worse than before. "Reckon I'll wait if it's all right with you."

"You do whatever you want, Marshal," the orderly said with no interest whatsoever, picking up a magazine and returning to the intimate revelations of the *Police Gazette*.

Longarm wandered out onto the porch. The air was moist and cool, and the sound of the rain—now that he was no longer being pelted by it—was a muted and rather pleasant drone.

He pulled out one of the agency trading post cigars and, with a skeptical grimace, lighted the thing.

"God, these things are rotten," he said to no one in particular. The crooks were, in fact, even worse than their price led one to expect. Maybe he should have taken the sutler up on that hemp rope after all. It likely would have tasted better than this.

"I don't think you can hold God responsible for anything that smells that bad," a voice said behind him.

Longarm turned, smiled, and extended his hand for a shake. "Reverend. I thought you were busy."

"Thomas told me you were out here. We weren't talking about anything that couldn't be interrupted. Come inside, please. Join us."

The "us" turned out to be the same crowd Longarm had met the day before, including the civilian teamster from Deadwood, Cale Rogers. Charles Prandel was there, as was the agency supply officer, Booth Watkins. Longarm would not have thought of them as a bunch of good old boys given to devotional meetings. But then what the hell did he know about devotional meetings anyway?

"Nice to see you again," Longarm said, and helped himself to a chair.

"My spies," Reverend MacNall said with a laugh, "tell me you've been up to the Crow camp. I hope Cloud Talker is being more forthcoming with you than he has been with me."

"Not likely," Longarm said. "Cloud Talker doesn't seem one to say all that much."

"That has been my experience too," the agent said. "Is there anything we can help you with?"

"You can tell me whatever it is you fellas know about the death o' John Jumps-the-Creek."

MacNall sighed. "I wish I knew more that I could tell you, Longarm. The tribal police reported it to me, of course. I only know the little they were able to ascertain. Apparently he was killed by one blow to the forehead, presumably a blow from a war club. An alarm was raised shortly before dawn of the

120

day in question when one of his wives went outside and found the body lying in front of his tent."

"Did the tribal police investigate the death?" Longarm asked.

"Of course. They looked into it immediately, but there were no witnesses. The judgment of all concerned is that the murderer is probably a member of the Crow nation, for reasons that I am sure you understand."

"That's what I keep hearing," Longarm agreed, "but I ain't seen any evidence that would point to the Crow."

"I know of no other reasons why a man of John Jumps-the-Creek's stature would be murdered," MacNall said.

"No? What about the tussle that's going on now over who will take his place as head shaman of the Piegan?"

MacNall rubbed his chin and frowned. "Really?"

"You didn't know 'bout that?"

"I must confess that I did not."

"The Piegan aren't only undecided about who will be their spiritual leader. There's also some question about who will become head man at the councils too."

"I thought among the Piegan both spiritual and administrative leadership was the same. And frankly, I assumed that Cloud Talker is next in the line of succession."

"John Jumps-the-Creek was shaman and head man too. That don't mean he'll be replaced by one man. Could be two. Usually is, in fact. John Jumper was unusually strong. His people respected him an' wanted to follow him. Cloud Talker doesn't have anything like John Jumps-the-Creek's force of character."

"That is interesting if true, Longarm. Are you sure of your information?"

Longarm shrugged. "How sure can anyone be who ain't

actually a Piegan himself? It's what I been told lately an' what I seen for myself in the past. That sure as hell—excuse me, Ames, I sometimes forget you're a reverend. What I meant to say is that I won't swear to anything. But I do believe it to be so until or unless I learn something to the contrary.''

"Of course all of this will be moot," MacNall said, "if open warfare breaks out on the reservation. If that happens there will have to be armed intervention, and the tribes will have to be separated somehow. Perhaps one of them moved to another agency where they will not be tempted to enter a cycle of recurring revenge and retaliation."

Rogers grunted and barked out a short, sharp little laugh. "If that happens, Ames, I want the haulage contract for the move."

"Always looking for the silver lining, aren't you, Cale?" MacNall said.

"You know me, Ames. If life gives me a pile of shit, I'll plant a garden and use it for fertilizer."

The agent threw his head back and roared. "I do like you, Cale. God knows that I do." Still smiling, he turned back to Longarm. "Is there anything we can do to help you, friend?"

"Keep your ears open. An' you might ask your tribal police to do the same."

"I will be glad to do that. We want to cooperate any way we possibly can. May I ask you something in return?"

"Of course."

"Do you think you have any realistic expectation that you can avert war here and talk the tribes into achieving an amicable peace?"

"I think there's a real good chance of it, Reverend. Tall Man will listen to me. We're old friends. An' if I can ever get Cloud Talker . . . and whoever else might emerge to lead the Piegan . . . if I can get them to sit an' smoke a pipe with me, then I think I got a real good chance to make sure nobody lights the fuse on the powder keg you got here.''

"Good,'' MacNall said with enthusiasm. "Be assured, sir, that you can count on our full cooperation. Anything at all, just let us know.''

"Thanks.'' Longarm took another puff on the vile cigar and looked outside. The rain was still falling, but not quite as heavily as before. "If you'll excuse me now, I think I wanta make a run for it before this mess gets any worse.''

MacNall walked with him onto the porch and shook Longarm's hand. "Good luck to you.''

"Thanks, Reverend. And to you.''

"Gray Buck,'' the agent called out, catching the attention of one of the Indian police who was taking refuge at the far end of the porch. "Fetch the marshal's horse, would you? Then I have an errand for you to run, please.''

The policeman bobbed his head and ran out into the rain, taking his precious—well, to him anyway—old Springfield .50–70 with him.

Chapter 25

It wasn't but a whoop and a holler from the agency head-quarters back to Tall Man's Crow camp, but the dreary, driz-zling rain made it seem further.

Rather than risk the horse's legs—Longarm had scant re-gard for the animal, actually—on the mud-slick ridge that he and Tall Man had come thundering across during their race, Longarm rode wide around it and splashed into the creek that meandered through the basin where the Upper Belle Fourche Intertribal Agency was laid out.

At least on a day like this he did not have to worry about the heavy-footed horse getting him wet. He was already wet to the skin. It was a good thing he had clothes on. Naked he most likely would have looked like a large, pink prune. He was thinking about the warmth he could expect to find in Tall Man's lodge and about the prospects of getting out of his sodden clothes. He hadn't brought baggage with him from Camp Beloit—the primary reason he wanted to get back there soon—but if nothing else, he could borrow a breechclout and blanket from Tall Man. Yellow Flowers could dry his wet garments by the fire tonight, and by morning he could set out warm and dry again. If the damned rain quit, that is. There was no sign yet of that, although in truth it had let up considerably. It—

Longarm's Stetson took flight, leaping high in the air and sailing over the horse's ears to land in the rain-dappled water of the creek.

Longarm bent low onto the animal's neck and took a firmer grip on the reins to keep the horse from bolting.

Even as he was busy doing that with his left hand his right was groping behind him in search of the butt of his Winchester.

Except, dammit, the Winchester, along with Longarm's own McClellan saddle, was back at the army post, and this borrowed rig had no carbine attached to it. Not even one of the stubby and ineffective little Springfield .45–55 cavalry carbines that were damned little improvement over the old .50–70 trapdoor conversions.

Somewhere back behind him—about at the top of the ridgeline, he guessed without actually seeing—he heard the dull, belated report of a muzzle blast. The sound was partially muffled by the rain and the moist, heavy air the rain caused, but Longarm had no trouble figuring out that some son of a bitch was back there shooting at him.

With no long gun to return the fire, Longarm was in what could best be described as a piss-poor position.

Turning around and charging uphill into the teeth of a rifleman with a solid rest to shoot from and a constantly diminishing range did not seem an especially bright idea to him.

And while he had nothing whatsoever against running the

hell away, that option would only expose his back to continued attempts by the rifleman to plant a bullet in the vicinity of Longarm's spine.

That choice was not particularly enticing either.

Longarm picked the third choice. He rolled off the horse's back and into the water.

At which point he discovered that he had been completely wrong about something.

It *was* possible to get wetter than he'd already been.

The creek wasn't just wet, it was almighty cold.

A second bullet came buzzing in just as Longarm came up spitting and sputtering and gasping for breath after momentarily disappearing beneath the water's surface.

White spray flew about two feet to Longarm's right, and the horse tried to pull away.

It was only then, actually, that Longarm noticed he still had a grip on one of the leather reins. The horse reared in terror and tried to bolt.

The hell with that. It might be a little tough on the horse, but that nine hundred pounds or so of hide and flesh was all the cover there was for several hundred yards in any direction, and Longarm wasn't about to turn loose of that rein.

He came to his feet, dripping water and shivering with cold but not really concerned about that at the moment. He hauled the horse back down on all four legs and turned it so that the animal was between him and the rifleman somewhere up there on the ridge.

The ambusher helped Longarm's spotting skills by firing again. A puff of white smoke bloomed high atop the crown of the ridge, and seconds later Longarm felt the horse flinch.

Longarm had only his revolver to return the fire, and there

was little chance he could score a hit at a distance of a hundred fifty yards or so.

On the other hand, just making the asshole nervous would be a help.

Longarm steadied his hand across the saddle and took careful aim, lining his sights on a point about a foot above where he thought the rifleman should be. He cocked the hammer manually and took a deep breath, let half of it out, and then slowly, gently applied just the least lick of pressure to the trigger of the big .44.

The Colt rocked in his hand and let out a satisfying bellow.

Mud and rock chips flew a good three feet wide of Longarm's mark and a couple feet low. So much for long-range marksmanship in the rain.

"Shit," he complained.

He stood there, huddled close behind the body of the horse, waiting for another telltale puff of gunsmoke to mark a target for him.

There was no other shot, however, and after several minutes it occurred to Longarm that he was having to hunker lower and lower in order to stay behind the horse.

The animal was sinking slowly to its knees. After a while the last of its endurance waned, and it rolled over into the creek with a huge splash.

"Shit," Longarm repeated.

He shoved his Colt back into its holster and stood over the dead horse, wondering if the sonuvabitch of a rifleman was still up there on that ridge waiting to pot him, wondering where his hat had floated to, wondering why in hell someone wanted to shoot him in the first place.

He didn't have answers to any of those questions, and after a bit he gave up wondering and turned to walk the rest of the way back to Tall Man's lodge.

Chapter 26

Longarm woke as completely as if he'd been doused with water cold from the creek. He had no idea what time it was. In the middle of the night, he suspected. The evening fire had burned down to coals with their red heat hidden beneath layers of dark ash. The lodge was dark, and all around him Longarm could hear the soft, slow breathing of people in sleep.

He sat up on the buffalo-robe bed and clutched his blanket close around his shoulders. He felt awkward and uncomfortable with no clothes, not even his drawers, on underneath the blanket.

Yellow Flowers, with Tall Man smirking in the background, had demanded that he shed everything down to the skin before they went to bed.

Longarm had protested. But only a little. His unwanted dip in the creek, to say nothing of the rain before it, had left him soaked and chilled and rather thoroughly miserable. He wanted to dry out as badly as Yellow Flowers insisted that he do, so after a token refusal he'd given in and handed over the clothing. All of it. Now his things were hanging on cords of twisted wild grass stems suspended along the inside wall of the lodge.

He reached over to feel of the nearest piece, and found it was not quite dry yet. He supposed that information should have told him about what time it was. But somehow he'd missed out on calculating time from the speed with which laundry dried.

Late. He was sure it was late. Beyond that he hadn't a clue.

He yawned and stood, slipping his feet into a pair of elderly and too-big moccasins of Tall Man's that Yellow Flowers had given him. His boots too were going through a drying-out process, this one involving hot sand that was poured into them and replaced every now and then with more sand that was fresh and dry, while the old, cold damp sand was discarded.

Still holding the blanket close around him, Longarm found a cigar and stooped to light it from the coals before taking it outside. The rum crooks had been as thoroughly drenched as Longarm and his garments, but it seemed that nothing could cause them serious damage. Hell, they were already so bad, who would recognize it if they got any worse.

Longarm took his blanket and his smoke and waddled—the moccasins were big enough to feel like buckets—out onto open ground away from the smells and the night noises of the sleeping Crow camp.

The aimless meandering eventually brought him back to the rock where he'd rested the night before, and he sat down there to finish his smoke.

A minute, no more than two, later he saw the approach of a pair of unearthly wraiths in the night.

Somehow, this time he was no longer surprised.

• • •

"I suppose you called me here," Longarm said by way of a greeting.

"Yes. Thank you for coming." Angelica smiled and took a seat beside him. The white dog licked his hand and wagged its tail and as before curled up at Longarm's feet.

Longarm didn't bother trying to argue the point with her. And hell, he didn't know why he'd come awake when he did and felt like taking a walk. Maybe she did.

"Who are you?" he asked.

"Angelica," she answered. "I told you that."

"Yeah, but Tall Man doesn't know you."

"He does not," Angelica agreed.

"Tall Man says he knows all his own people."

"Yes, I would expect him to. There are not so very many."

"But he doesn't know you."

"No."

"Why not?"

Angelica smiled. God, he could look at that smile every morning and not get tired of it. Not in a lifetime of close looking. "I am not of Tall Man's people," she said.

"Are you tryin' to tell me you're some kinda . . . I dunno . . . some kinda spirit? Or something?"

Angelica threw her head back and laughed. It was like a chorus of bells chiming. Pure music. "You are funny, Long Arm."

"I wasn't tryin' to be," he admitted.

"No. That is why it is so funny."

"If you don't belong here . . ."

She laughed again and touched his wrist. Longarm was sure the girl's flesh was electrically charged. It had to be to have that much of an impact on him. "I do belong here, Long Arm. But in the other village."

130

"Huh?"

"I am Piegan, Long Arm. Not Crow."

"But . . ."

"Because I walk here in the night you think I must be of the Crow people? No, Long Arm. I walk here because this is where the spirits guide my feet. I walk here because you have come to help our people. Both our peoples, the Piegan and the Crow. The spirits tell me I must speak with you. And so I do as I am guided."

"These spirits of yours," he said. "Do they happen to know what happened to John Jumps-the-Creek?"

"They know," Angelica said.

"What, then?"

She shook her head. "I said the spirits know. This is true. I did not say they have told me."

"But they told you about me."

"Yes. You are to be a . . . what is the word in your language . . . the tool?" She thought for a moment, then smiled. "The instrument. That is the correct way to say. You are the instrument to save our peoples with the truth."

"If I only knew the truth," Longarm said.

"You will. When the time comes, Long Arm, the spirit wolf will help you to know what is true."

"The spirit wolf," he repeated, bending down to scratch the dog behind its ears. The dog wagged its tail and wriggled and when he quit scratching, turned to lick his hand. Some wolf, he thought. About as ferocious, this one, as a young cottontail rabbit.

"Do you find this so very hard to accept?" the pretty girl asked.

"To tell you the truth . . . yeah. I do find it a bit much to swallow."

She shrugged, her eyes twinkling. "Chew on it, Long Arm."

"Smart aleck, ain't you?"

"Sometimes," she agreed. "Sometimes, yes."

"Smart enough to know that I'm taken with you?"

"Yes, Long Arm. I know that you are. I too feel the thing that is between us."

"I don't suppose. . . ."

Angelica shook her head. "No, Long Arm. I am a virgin. I must remain a virgin. If I allow a man to have my body, the spirits will take back the gifts that were given to me. I will no longer be able to serve my people."

He swallowed. Hard. There was something about this girl. . . .

"Pity," he drawled.

"Yes. It is." She touched his wrist again, and the sensation raced up his arm and down his spine. He shivered. And positively ached from wanting her.

Angelica turned her face away from him and stiffened. "Please, Long Arm. Do not do this to me."

"Do?"

"The thing that you are thinking. I want it too. Help me, Long Arm. Please."

He stood. He took her hand and lifted her gently to her feet.

He bent and tasted of her lips. Her breath was sweet and her lips soft as down and warm as sunshine. He felt a shudder run through her. "You," he said.

"You," she repeated.

He kissed her again. Again he felt the shuddering, jolting impact of it deep in her flesh. She trembled, and he realized that as much as she enjoyed his touch, she was truly, genuinely frightened now.

Longarm reluctantly let go of her and took a deliberate step backward. "I think I . . ."

Angelica laid a fingertip to his lips to silence him. She stood silent and motionless, looking at him, for long heartbeats.

Then she turned and ran away into the night.

The ghostly white dog stood at Longarm's knee watching her nearly out of sight. Then it too burst into motion, racing after her.

Not until both the girl and the dog were long out of view did Longarm turn and make his way back down to the Crow camp and Tall Man's lodge.

Chapter 27

To judge by the morning, there might not have been any rain to mar the weather in more than a month. Come morning the sky was purest blue and the horizon empty of clouds. Longarm gave Tall Man a rum crook. Giving the damn things away beat hell out of smoking them, but so far Tall Man hadn't taken the bait and reciprocated by offering Longarm one of the cheroots he had lost to him in the horse race. Then Longarm lighted a crook for himself as well. Having the night to dry out hadn't improved the taste of the ugly little cigars the least little bit.

"You will go to the soldiers now?" Tall Man asked.

"Soon," Longarm said. "I have to stop and get the saddle off that horse I left in the creek yesterday. It's bad enough I cost the man a horse. I don't wanta leave him without a saddle too."

"You will need a horse to ride. You will take my painted war pony."

Longarm shook his head. "I can't let you risk him, my friend. If somebody has it in for me, I don't wanta take a chance on them shooting your best horse too. But I'd like to have the borrow of the chestnut again." Longarm grinned. "He's a slow sonuvabitch, but at least I know he won't trip over himself and fall down."

"Looks fast, though," Tall Man said with great satisfaction.

Longarm laughed. "You find the chestnut if you like. I'll go fetch the saddle an' be back shortly."

"Wait." Tall Man called out to some of his warriors who were lounging nearby around the remains of the breakfast fires, and spoke to them at length. The men scattered, only to return moments later carrying an improbable assortment of muskets, battered old Spencer carbines, rusty muzzle-loaders, and even a couple of Henry repeating rifles. There was not a gun among them that Longarm would have felt safe pulling the trigger of, but the Crow seemed proud enough of their ragtag arsenal.

"We will go now," Tall Man said. "Burned Pot will bring the horse to you."

"What's this? You think I need an escort?"

"Does Longarm have magic to turn bullets from his flesh? No? I think you need an escort, yes."

Longarm looked over toward the low ridge where the rifleman had been yesterday. And decided not to argue with his friend Tall Man.

The bunch of them, more than a dozen strong, walked through grass and wildflowers to the creek where the army horse lay dead half in the water and half out. Longarm and Tall Man and two of the Crow stopped there. The rest of the warriors continued on to the top of the ridge and beyond it.

There would be no ambush today. Not, at least, from that direction.

At Tall Man's command the two Crow stripped the tack off the horse and piled it on the creek bank to begin drying in the early morning sun.

"There is one more thing, I think," Tall Man suggested.

"Uh-huh. Reckon there is at that."

Tall Man took out his knife and motioned to the two warriors, who rolled the dead horse over onto its other side. There were two bullet holes marring the animal's hide, one in the chest cavity—that would have been the slug that killed the horse—and the other in the rump. "This one," Tall Man said, pointing to the wound in the animal's butt. He knelt, unmindful of the cold water that swirled around his knees, and began cutting into the wound channel the bullet had made in its passage.

While Tall Man was busy hunting for a speck of lead inside half a ton of cold, decaying horseflesh, Longarm wandered downstream in search of his Stetson. It must have floated far or else someone else had already found it and picked it up this morning, because there was no sign of the hat. Dammit!

By the time Longarm returned to the site of yesterday's ambush, Tall Man and most of his men were squatting around a small fire on the creek bank roasting strips of dark red meat. And the rump of the horse had been laid open much further than seemed necessary just for the removal of a bullet.

Not that Longarm had anything against eating horse meat. Hell, the animal hadn't been anybody's pet, least of all his. "Did you find it?" he asked.

Tall Man grunted and stood, handing over an only slightly distorted lump of gray lead.

"Fifty-seventy," Longarm said.

"The Piegan carry this size ball," Tall Man offered.

"So do a helluva lot of others. Including prob'ly half your warriors." After the Springfield Armory converted to making the much more efficient and higher-quality .45–70 models, and the army had finally stopped distributing arms and ammunition in the old .50–70 caliber, there had been, literally, tens of thousands of the obsolete models to dispose of. Virtually every state and territorial militia in the country was now armed with the old guns. Thousands more were sold to the military forces—or perhaps as often to rebel groups—in foreign nations. And more tens of thousands were distributed to almost anyone who wanted them, whether homesteaders seeking to protect their farms or Indian tribes wanting breechloaders for the pursuit of buffalo. Or nowadays, for "hunting" and slaughtering from horseback the beef rations delivered to them on the hoof.

Anyway, it was not exactly a startling discovery to learn that yesterday's shooter had been armed with a .50–70. Long-arm would have been amazed, actually, if they'd found anything else.

But he'd wanted to know, regardless.

At some point while he'd been wandering downstream Burned Pot had brought the chestnut over from the horse herd, and someone had already saddled it with the things taken off the army horse.

Longarm shook hands with Tall Man and thanked the Crow warriors, then mounted the slow but pretty chestnut and reined it toward Camp Beloit.

Chapter 28

Longarm was downright proud of himself. He made it back to Camp Beloit without a guide, over a route he'd only traveled once before, and did it without ever getting lost. A trifle confused now and then, but never actually lost.

In fact he managed to home in on the place and make his approach a single valley away from the direct route. Which, under the circumstances, he considered to be a pretty fair performance.

The chestnut proved to be a first-class road horse, and the day was bright and warm and fair. Longarm found himself in a genuine good mood as he came down toward the ugly little army camp.

He saw a small hunting party on the ridge top to his left and waved to them, receiving a friendly wave in return. Indians, he thought, although he could not make out which tribe they belonged to. He did question their choice of a place from which to look for game. Surely they had to know how close the soldiers at Beloit were, and just as surely the presence of the soldiers would scare game away. Still, that was only an assumption. Perhaps those fellows up on the ridge knew something Longarm didn't. Or then again, maybe it wasn't game they were waiting for but some soldier who would sell them whiskey or other contraband. Fortunately for Longarm, it was not a problem that was his to worry about.

He rode on, and within a half hour reached Captain Wingate's headquarters.

"Longarm. Welcome. Where is the horse . . . never mind, you can explain later. Get down, man. Come inside here. There is someone I want you to meet. Remember when that fellow said a civilian hired a rig for transportation out here? Do you remember that?" The officer laughed. He seemed quite excited about whatever this was. "Come inside now. Hurry."

Longarm stepped down off the chestnut and handed his reins to Wingate's orderly.

"Christ, I almost took you for an Indian when you were coming in," the one-time brevet colonel said, "dressed the way you are."

Longarm himself had as good as forgotten his rather bizarre costume, which consisted more of items borrowed from Tall Man than his own clothing, still damp from his swim the day before. And of course he had no hat. Dammit. A man accustomed to wearing a hat is unduly annoyed by sunlight in the eyes, and Longarm had been blinking and complaining to himself the whole way down from the agency.

"Here. Go ahead inside," Wingate said, taking him by the elbow and propelling him through the tent flap into the shade and relative cool within.

Longarm stopped dead in his tracks.

"Deputy Marshal Long, I would like you to meet—"

It was the randy, skinny, insatiable blonde with the hot pussy and deep mouth who'd been his traveling companion on the stagecoach north.

"—my wife Amanda," Wingate concluded.

It was a good thing Longarm didn't have false teeth. He would have coughed them right out of his mouth and into the dirt if he had.

As it was, he bent double in a fit of wheezing and hacking meant to cover his confusion.

Amanda Wingate, on the other hand, seemed quite thoroughly at ease with the situation of seeing her husband and a recent lover together. But hell, it likely was a situation she'd faced often enough before now, Longarm thought uncharitably.

After all, the woman was the one who'd practically raped him.

And come to think of it, she'd gotten into Deadwood at the exact same time he had, but it had taken her a couple of extra days to make it out here to join her husband. The logical explanation for that was that she'd wanted to see what kind of males she could find to suck dry—and he was thinking of that in the sense of a black widow spider, not as the term sometimes related to the pleasures of sex—before she drove out here to join Captain Wingate.

Longarm managed to regain control of himself, and made a small bow while Wingate completed the formalities of introduction.

"Pleased to meet you, ma'am."

"Likewise, I am sure, sir." Amanda Wingate laughed and fluttered her eyelashes shamelessly.

"I believe you will find, Longarm, that my Amanda has a

140

perfectly devilish sense of humor. She pretends to be the flirt, you see, but she is really the sweetest lamb possible, and I do love her most dearly.''

"Yes, I can see that you do," Longarm said.

Poor sonuvabitch, he was thinking. It was a good thing a cuckold's horns weren't visible, or Wingate would have been wearing a trophy-sized rack on his head.

"You will join us for dinner, sir?" Mrs. Wingate suggested.

"It would be my pleasure, ma'am."

"Sir?" The orderly, or another just like him, was peering in through the headquarters tent flap.

"What is it, Boatwright?" the commanding officer asked.

"Wagons coming, sir. Should be that load of supplies you've been looking for. You said you wanted to know."

"Excellent," Wingate said with a smile. "Thank you."

The orderly saluted, the gesture perfunctory and poorly executed, and withdrew.

"If you two would excuse me," Wingate said, "I have to see to the unloading and distribution of these supplies."

Longarm touched his forehead—he wasn't wearing a hat but had forgotten that small detail at the moment—and hurried out on Wingate's heels. He suspected it would be a good idea for him to avoid spending any time alone with the lovely Amanda lest she bring up things best forgotten now that she was back in the company of her husband.

Besides, there is always something delightfully fascinating about watching others hard at work.

Chapter 29

Pale moonlight entered the small, low-ceilinged dugout as the green elk hide nailed over the door was pulled aside.

There was light to see by for only a few seconds. Then a body filled the space, and quickly thereafter the elk skin dropped back into place, closing out the moonlight.

Longarm was not startled. Hell, he'd been more or less expecting the visit.

He heard the faint sound of cloth rustling in the silence of the night. He'd heard the same thing before. This time, though, it was not something he'd been looking forward to. If there had been a lock on the door into the dugout, he would have bolted it. Unfortunately, there hadn't been.

"Go away," Longarm said, his voice low. "Go back to your husband, Mrs. Wingate."

"What? No hello kiss, Marshal? And after all we've been to each other. Imagine that."

"Like I said, ma'am. Go back to your husband. I don't want you here."

"You wanted me before, though. Didn't you?"

"An' I gave you what you wanted too, but that's past now. Leave it be."

"But dear, I didn't know then that I was fucking a real United States marshal. You should have told me. It is so exciting, darling, thinking about all those vicious criminals you've brought to justice. Have you ever had to shoot any of them? Tell me what it feels like to kill a man."

"I wouldn't know. I've never had to shoot nobody."

"Now why is it that I have the feeling you are lying to me, darling?" She laughed, her voice brittle in the night. He felt her come nearer to him, although it was so dark inside the dugout that he could not see her. "Can you believe it, dear? That was one of the reasons why I chose to marry Tom. He looked so dashing in his uniform. So . . . martial." She laughed again. "A strange twist, isn't that? My martial lover has been a huge disappointment. But not my marshal. You were quite good, you know. You know how to please a woman. Poor Tom doesn't know anything more about women than he does about killing. A store clerk, that's all Tom is. A dull and dreary little store clerk. And he hardly knows what to do with that pathetic little thing between his legs. Now you, darling, that is a hammer you have. And you know how to use it. It makes me wet just thinking about how it was being with you. Why, you are the best I've had in . . . months and months. Truly you are."

Longarm felt the touch of her hand. Finding his waist. His crotch. Slipping inside his trousers to cup and tickle his balls and gently squeeze his cock.

"So big," Mrs. Wingate whispered as she continued to

stroke him. "I love that, you know. Is it true that in Mexico they put on performances where ponies fuck human whores? Have you ever seen any such thing? Do you know how excited it makes me feel, thinking about having a cock that size rammed into me? Tell me they really do that sort of thing, dear, and I'll head straight for Mexico when I leave here."

"Can I ask you something?"

"Of course, dear. I have no secrets from you." She laughed. "Well, hardly any. And none at all that are important."

"Why'd you come here now? I mean, you've already as good as said your marriage was a mistake. I know good an' well you don't lack for male companionship. So why'd you come here in the first place?"

"But darling, didn't I tell you? Tommy's family is very rich. I have to see about my allowance, dear. I need an increase. So I'll spend a month or so letting Tom paw my body, and then when I have what I need I'll go down to Mexico and find out if they really do that down there. Tell me, won't you? Tell me the truth."

"I don't know if they do any such a thing," Longarm lied. "Don't care neither." That was certainly the truth.

"Oh, this feels so nice," she cooed as she stroked and pulled at his erection.

"Go back to your husband, Mrs. Wingate. I don't want you."

"You're lying now, dear. I can feel in this tool of yours that you want me. Your prick wants me, dear, even if you think you don't. Your prick knows. Always trust your prick, darling. It won't lead you astray."

Now there was some sage advice, Longarm thought. Sure. You bet. "Go back to your husband now. Please."

"What for, dear? Poor Tommy is already worn out. Can

144

you believe it? One, two little climaxes and he's done for. He is in his bed snoring up a proper storm. And so satisfied that he's sleeping with a smile on his silly face. He didn't give me near enough, dear. So I thought I would come visit you and get the rest of what I need tonight.''

"No, thanks. I'm not interested.''

"Of course you are, dearest.'' She squeezed his cock. Rather sharply this time. "Besides, if you don't do what I want, darling, I just may scream and burst into such big old tears that anyone, just anyone, would have to believe that you tried to molest me.''

Longarm took her hand and pulled it away from his pecker. "Leave me alone, damn you.''

"I'll scream. Believe me, dear, I can wake up this entire camp. What will they think, hmm? You could go to one of those prisons you've helped to fill with those horrid, nasty little bad men. You might even hang for trying to rape me. Oh, doesn't that make you all hot and horny just thinking about it? You could die for me, love. Even if you don't especially want to.''

"Mrs. Wingate, whyn't you go fuck yourself if it's a fuck you want so awful bad.''

"I'm warning you, Marshal. I'll scream. I will.''

"Go ahead.''

"What?''

"I said go ahead. Scream your fool head off. If anybody hears you . . . an' I doubt that they would, seeing as how we're buried under three, four feet o' dirt and sod in this dugout . . . but even if somebody does hear you, they wouldn't hang me without a court-martial. An' just think what it'd do to your reputation when my friend Quentin Cooper, the stage driver, testifies about you giving me blow jobs on the roof of the coach on the way up here. You thought he didn't notice? Hell, Quint thought that was one of the funniest things he ever saw, you on your knees with your face full of cock. And once Quint testifies, *darling* . . . just think what effect that will have on Colonel Wingate's family." His voice hardened. "Think what effect Quint's testimony will have on your allowance."

"You wouldn't!" she gasped.

"Scream, bitch. That's the only way you'll really find out if I'm running a bluff. You wanta make sure you're heard? Step outside before you yell. Make sure someone comes to rescue you. Then see how it works out from there."

"You bastard."

"You bitch."

"I hate your guts, damn you."

"Seems fair enough since I don't have a helluva lot of regard for you neither."

"God, I want you. Fuck me. I'll leave you alone after that, dear. I promise. But I'm so hot I'll burn up if I can't get your cock inside me right now."

"Sorry. Not interested."

"Liar."

But in fact he was not. His erection had subsided by now, and no amount of kneading and pulling would bring it back. Mrs. Wingate dropped to her knees and tried to blow him again, sucking and making wet, gobbling noises in her anxiety to prove that she could command pleasure from him.

Her efforts were in vain. All she managed to do was to make him wet with her saliva. Longarm's pecker remained flaccid and limp in her mouth.

For one awful moment he thought she was going to bite in her frustration, but fortunately she did not think of that. He was sure the only reason she would refrain, however, was because it did not occur to her. Restraint . . . and for that matter, rational behavior . . . did not seem to be the lady's long suit.

"Bastard," she spat at him when finally she let his prick slide out from between her lips.

"Bitch."

She stood and slapped him across the face. Hard.

Longarm slapped her back.

"Oh, God, yes. Do that again."

Thoroughly disgusted, Longarm spun the woman around, planted a foot in her backside, and gave her a shove that sent her tumbling through the doorway and out into the moonlit night.

He found her hat and the much-remembered duster on the floor, gathered them into a clumsy wad, and threw them out too.

The woman picked herself up and stood there for a moment glaring at him, her expression one of unalloyed hatred.

For half a heartbeat he was convinced she was going to do it, that she was going to scream and cry rape after all.

But she had too much to lose.

After a time she bent—she really was one fine-looking figure of a woman, damn her—and retrieved the hat and duster. She yanked them on and stormed away into the night.

Longarm sighed with relief as he turned back toward the borrowed bed in what passed for Visiting Officers' Quarters at Camp Beloit.

Chapter 30

"Are you sure you won't stay, Longarm? Mrs. Wingate was saying only last evening what a nice man you seem. I know she would be pleased to entertain you. I, uh, I have rather a lot that I must do right now. To tell you the truth, Longarm, it would be something of a favor to me if you could stay longer. Keeping Amanda amused, don't you see, so that I can get my work done."

"I'd like to, Tom, but I have to get back to the agency and see can I keep things calm." Longarm finished tying his gear onto the saddle—his own saddle this time, thank goodness—and dropped the stirrup in place. "If the Piegan an' Crow go at each other, you'll have a lot more to do than the administrative stuff here."

"I suppose that is true."

"Thanks for the hospitality," Longarm said. He smiled and added, "An' thanks for the hat." It was no Stetson, but the officer had come up with an old Kossuth—probably obtained from the camp trash heap—that he'd given to Longarm. The sloppy, floppy rag of black wool felt was no substitute for Longarm's favored brown fur felt. But it was indisputably better than nothing, and so Longarm was pleased to have it.

Longarm swung onto the back of the chestnut pony, and gave the fractious animal a few moments to settle down. The horse was not accustomed to a bit and bridle, Indians generally preferring to use a single rein knotted around the lower jaw to control their mounts. Longarm could ride with that arrangement in a pinch, but it was not comfortable for him. And if one of the two had to be in discomfort on this score, he figured it could just damn well be the horse. He did his part by giving up his comfort for the horse's when it came to a choice of saddle, the McClellan being a fine fit for a horse's back but a real ball-buster for the human rider who had to suffer on the upper side of the thing.

"Any idea when you'll be back?" Wingate asked.

"None," Longarm admitted. "But I'll make it a point to come back through an' bring you up to date even if things go well. If they don't, well, you an' your boys can pick up the pieces an' ship me back to Denver." If there's any of you left either, Longarm thought to himself, but refrained from saying aloud.

"Now there is a voice of confidence," the captain said with a small smile.

"If I can't be confident, Tom, I can at least be practical." Longarm leaned down to shake the man's hand, then backed the chestnut a few paces and lightly touched the brim of the ugly Kossuth hat. "Come a-runnin' if you hear the sound of guns, Tom."

"I'd be happier if you can keep those guns quiet, Longarm."

Longarm nodded and reined the chestnut north, toward the Indian agency.

Yellow Flowers stepped out of the lodge, took one look at Longarm, and fainted dead away.

It was, Longarm thought, an unusual form of greeting, to say the very least.

He jumped down off the chestnut and dropped his reins to ground-tie the animal. That was usually an invitation for a horse to declare itself free, but in this case he didn't much give a shit. He wanted to see to Yellow Flowers. Besides, if the chestnut did run away, it was not likely to run any further than the Crow horse herd, and there would be no real harm in that.

Longarm knelt beside Yellow Flowers and rubbed her cheeks and her wrists the way he'd seen others try to revive stricken ladies. "Yellow Flowers? Are you all right? Talk to me, Yellow Flowers. What's wrong? Where's Tall Man?" Longarm's initial thought was that Tall Man had been killed and the tribes were on the brink of war. That or . . . God knows what other possibilities could exist. "Yellow Flowers?"

Burned Pot and a gaggle of little girls had come outside too by now, and were gathered close around, but none of them appeared to speak any English. And there was no sign of Tall Man in his own lodge. That was damn-all worrisome.

"Yellow Flowers?"

Burned Pot brought out a wet cloth and bathed Yellow Flowers' face with it. A moment more and the older wife of Tall Man sneezed. Then opened her eyes.

Her eyes went immediately wide again, and for a moment Longarm thought she would pass out for the second time in as many minutes. But she did not. She groaned a little and wriggled about on the grass, and soon struggled to sit upright. He helped her so that she was sitting on the beaten earth at the entry to the lodge.

"What is it, Yellow Flowers? What's wrong?"

"You are not a spirit, Longarm? You have not come to take me with you to the spirit world?"

"No, Yellow Flowers, I'm the same as always. An' the only place I come from is the army camp down south of here. Now will you please tell me—"

"Word came to us that Longarm was dead. It is said you were killed in the hills to the west. Your body is being brought to Agent MacNall at the place of the white men's houses. Tall Man went there to claim the body of his friend and to mourn."

"Did Tall Man take his gun?"

Yellow Flowers hesitated.

"Yellow Flowers. Please!"

Reluctantly she nodded. "Yes, Longarm. My husband took his gun and rode his best war horse when he went to see what the Piegan did to his friend."

"Christ!" Longarm erupted.

He came to his feet and spun away, not even taking time to speak a word of good-bye, nor one of warning, to Yellow Flowers and Burned Pot.

He ran for the chestnut—thank goodness the horse hadn't wandered away trailing the reins—and vaulted into the saddle, driving his spurs into the animal's flanks before he even had time enough to take a good seat.

There was no time to waste, dammit.

Chapter 31

The chestnut had no speed, but by God it had heart. Longarm had to give the creature that much. It never quit on him.

He thundered through the creek, silvery plumes of water arcing high, and on across. Up the low ridge and down the other side.

The horse gave him everything that was in it. The run might well have broken its wind. But the horse's great heart was strong, and it charged with everything it had for every foot of the distance.

And a fine thing that was because Longarm got there barely in time.

Tall Man was outside the agency headquarters, surrounded by Piegan tribal police and engaged in a silent fury of hand-to-hand combat with at least eight of the snotty sons of bitches.

Tall Man's rifle and ceremonial war club had been stripped away from him, and the Blood policemen were busy administering a thumping, kicking, clubbing beating to the lone Crow leader.

Blood coated Tall Man's face and neck and chest, and one eye was swollen shut so that he could not see to even try to ward off the blows that rained down on him from that blind side.

Tall Man was no more of a quitter than his chestnut traveling horse, however, and every time one of the Piegan landed a blow, Tall Man lashed out in swift, if ineffective, retaliation.

Longarm got the impression the Piegan were enjoying themselves. Taking their time about cutting down this ancient enemy. They wanted to humiliate him, Longarm suspected.

All but one of the bastards.

That one was not taking an active part in the vicious pummeling. He was standing back, watching, waiting. And when he felt sure he had been forgotten, the short, stocky policeman reached beneath his tunic and brought out a Hudson's Bay butcher knife, the old familiar model with the ten-inch blade and an excellent temper to the steel.

The Piegan was maneuvering himself to a position immediately behind Tall Man when Longarm saw what he was up to and took a hand.

Longarm did not waste time dismounting from the chestnut and charging the Piegan. He simply pointed the tiring horse at the police officer and slammed into the sonuvabitch.

The Piegan flew in one direction and his knife in another, and Longarm threw himself off the horse and into the middle of the fray.

"You, back off. You, over there. You and you and you, grab this cowardly back-stabbing cocksucker and put him in irons. No, goddammit, don't look at me like that. Do what I tell you. Right damn now. That's right. In manacles. The man

153

tried to commit a murder. I witnessed the crime, and he's my prisoner. Do you want to argue the point with me and go to prison with him? Then haul out your cuffs and put them on that man right damn now. *Do* it!''

Longarm's tone of voice left no room for argument.

It helped, of course, that the Piegan cops were so surprised by his sudden, unnerving appearance among them.

But then after all, as far as they knew, they were being confronted by a ghost. And a furious one at that.

Not too many Indians wanted to piss off ghosts. This bunch certainly did not.

Longarm helped Tall Man to his feet while the Piegan police took one of their own into custody and snapped steel bracelets onto him.

While all that was going on, the Reverend MacNall came outside to inquire about the commotion.

He too had heard the news about Longarm's death. Obviously so. When he saw Longarm standing there trying to mop some of the blood off Tall Man, MacNall stopped stock still and gaped. ''I thought . . .''

''So did everybody else, I reckon,'' Longarm said.

''But how did you . . . I mean, thank goodness you . . . I don't know exactly what I do mean. But God, I'm glad to see you alive and well.''

''You ain't the only one can say that, Reverend. Believe me.''

''You men,'' MacNall snapped at the Piegan coppers. ''What is the meaning of this trouble here?''

One of the policemen stammered out something and pointed to the one Longarm had placed under arrest.

''Is that necessary, Longarm?''

''It is, sir.'' Longarm explained what the Piegan tried to do.

"I saw it with my own eyes, Reverend. There's no doubt what he was up to." Longarm retrieved the knife from the ground. It had fallen against the side wall of the agency headquarters building. Close up the weapon looked every bit as nasty as it was. "If he'd put this in Tall Man's back, Reverend, there wouldn't have been no way to avoid these tribes going to war, sir. Think about that."

MacNall scowled and said something to the policeman in his own tongue. It was a gift Longarm hadn't known the reverend possessed and one Longarm wished he had. But then some people have a way with languages. And some have to struggle just trying to get along in one. Longarm found himself more at that end of the scale of possibilities than the other.

"I've ordered this man to be locked up, Longarm. You can take your prisoner any time you want him."

"Thank you, Reverend."

"As for this other business . . ."

"Yes, sir?"

"We still don't know much about your murder, do we?"

Despite the seriousness of the moment—or what could have been a deadly seriousness anyway had Longarm not intervened in time—Reverend MacNall looked somewhat amused when he mentioned Longarm's murder to the purported victim.

"I got to admit one thing to you," Longarm said, his voice solemn.

"Yes?"

"I'm gonna be real disturbed if I find out that it's true."

MacNall threw his head back and laughed openly, and Tall Man joined him.

Chapter 32

Another contingent of Piegan tribal police, three of them, brought in the body that was supposed to have been Longarm's.

The reason for the confusion was cleared up as soon as the people gathered at the agency headquarters saw the dead man.

He was an Indian. No question about that. But he was wearing a tweed coat, an ancient and ragged thing, but one which at a distance would appear remarkably similar to Longarm's normal clothing. And much more to the point, the dead man had been wearing Longarm's flat-crowned, snuff-brown Stetson hat. The one that Longarm hadn't been able to find after it floated downstream in the creek.

He did not now want the hat back. Not to wear again anyway, although it might still have some utilitarian value as evidence in a murder investigation.

The Stetson had been shot twice. Once off Longarm's head, the second time while this dead Indian was wearing it. Now the hat had been crushed—probably stepped on by one or more horses would be Longarm's guess—and was stiff with caked, dry blood and with other, even less pleasant-looking stuff.

The Indian who had been unfortunate enough to find the hat and wear it had been shot through the head by a large-caliber slug. Brain matter, darkening as it dried and hardened, was coated thick inside the crown of the expensive hat, and the fine beaver-fur felt was sodden with the man's spilled blood.

No, Longarm would not want his hat back. Not after a dozen cleanings would he want to put the thing on his head again.

But the Stetson told him volumes about the fate of the Indian who'd been wearing it.

"Poor son of a bitch," Longarm said. "Anybody know who he is?"

"He is not Crow," Tall Man said.

"I've seen him before," the Reverend MacNall said. "He's Piegan. I don't recall his name."

"Short Tail Rabbit," one of the policemen said. "He is one who wished to lead our people in council."

"Yes, of course," MacNall said. "I remember him now. Bright fellow and a good speaker. One of Cloud Talker's opponents in the quest for control of the tribe."

The policeman nodded.

"You know," MacNall mused aloud, "my first thought was that Short Tail Rabbit was mistaken for our friend Longarm and killed by accident. But now . . ."

It was an interesting theory anyway, Longarm thought. "Anybody know where Cloud Talker is?"

MacNall shook his head. Tall Man did not bother to answer.

It was safe enough to assume that he would neither know nor care much about the whereabouts, or the well-being, of the Piegan leader.

If, that is, Cloud Talker did indeed prove to be the leader of his people that he'd positioned himself to become.

"Anybody seen Cloud Talker today?" Longarm asked of no one in particular.

There were no responses. Apparently no one had.

"I think," Longarm said, "I'd best go find him an' have a talk with him. Any suggestions, anyone?"

"No," the agent said, "but if you don't mind, friend, I would like to send a police escort with you. Just, um, in case."

"In case of exactly what, Reverend?"

MacNall shrugged. And elected not to elaborate, possibly because of the Indians who were listening in to the conversation.

The agent said something to the Piegan policeman who seemed to be in charge, and that officer nodded to the trio of police who had just brought in the body of Short Tail Rabbit. "These men will go with you, Longarm, and keep an eye on your back."

"I appreciate that." It occurred to Longarm that yesterday when he'd waved to that "hunting party" on the ridge top when he was riding into Camp Beloit, he might well have been waving to a band of hunters who were hunting *him*. It seemed more than merely possible that they were fooled into letting him pass because he was bareheaded at the time and riding a Crow pony. They might simply have failed to recognize him from afar, just as someone mistook Short Tail Rabbit for Deputy Marshal Custis Long.

Unless MacNall was right, and Short Tail Rabbit's death

was a deliberate attempt by Cloud Talker to eliminate a political rival.

Or then again, Longarm speculated, both those possibilities could be true. One would not necessarily rule out the other. The "hunters" could have failed to recognize Longarm *and* Cloud Talker could have taken advantage of Short Tail Rabbit's wearing of Longarm's Stetson to shoot him and divert suspicion from himself.

And Hell might freeze over before tomorrow's sunrise too. Sometimes a man could think so damn much that all he accomplished was to tie himself in knots, Longarm knew.

The one thing Longarm was sure of right now was that he wanted to locate Cloud Talker and have a word with the man.

"You boys need to change to fresh horses before we start out? No? Then let's ride, fellas. Let's see can we find Cloud Talker before nightfall. Tall Man, I'll be back to spend tonight in your lodge if I can. If not, then I reckon I'll see you tomorrow." Longarm touched the brim of his old Kossuth—the thing didn't seem quite so nasty-looking in comparison with the current state of his Stetson—as an informal salute to Reverend MacNall, and swung into his saddle again.

He did want to have a word with Cloud Talker. And quick, before there were any more bodies around here, what with first John Jumps-the-Creek and now Short Tail Rabbit dead.

Very many more bodies and the Piegan nation, or anyway this band of it, would find itself without leadership altogether.

Chapter 33

It occurred to Longarm—somewhat too late to do anything about it—that he should have asked MacNall to send along someone who spoke some English. As it was, it looked like none of his escorts could speak a word of it.

They were making themselves clear enough in spite of that. What with gesturing and jabbering and pointing the way, they made it plain that they wanted Longarm to go with them to the spot where they'd found Short Tail Rabbit and then start the search for Cloud Talker from there.

It wasn't exactly the way Longarm might have chosen to handle it. But it could have been worse, he supposed.

And since he couldn't argue with them anyway, neither side being able to understand a word of what the other was saying, he gave in and went where the three Piegan policemen indicated.

They rode west from the agency, crossed the creek and the adjacent drainage, and entered a chain of low, grassy hills. In the distance Longarm could see the dark humps of some pine-covered bluffs reminiscent of the Black Hills. Except these hills up here did not have gold in them. Longarm was damn well positive about that. They wouldn't have been given to the Indians if they were worth anything.

They had gone seven, maybe eight miles when the Piegan cops pointed down to a thin trickle of water gleaming bright silver in the slanting afternoon sunlight. Again using broadly dramatic gestures, the tribal police indicated that this was where Short Tail Rabbit had met his demise.

The Piegan fell into single file behind Longarm as he let the chestnut pick its way down the shallow slope toward the murder site.

As they came close the horse began to fidget and blow snot, no doubt smelling blood there. Longarm shortened his rein and slipped his feet back in the stirrups until he barely had his toes on the irons.

It was not, however, the chestnut he was thinking about.

As Longarm's mount reached the tiny rill and gathered itself to jump across, Longarm heard the sound he'd been expecting.

He threw himself off the chestnut, striking the ground already in a roll and coming up with his Colt in his hand.

Behind him—behind where he'd just been actually—a .50–70 Springfield roared, and a slug the size of a grown man's thumb sizzled a foot or so above Longarm's saddle. His empty saddle.

The sharper, lighter bark of Longarm's Colt followed so fast behind the report of the rifle that the two sounds were almost as one, the six-gun's fire virtually an extension of the sound of the rifle shot.

One very amazed Piegan warrior took Longarm's bullet low in the throat. The policeman had time for his eyes to flash wide open in horror. Then he was driven backward off the seat pad of his pony to fall with a drenching splash into the creek, Springfield flying in one direction and his cavalry-style campaign hat in another.

Longarm did not take time to admire his work, however. He swung the muzzle of the Colt toward the next man in line, but before Longarm could pull the trigger that policeman too was driven backward off his horse.

The third warrior was unseated almost in the same instant, and Longarm of a sudden had no more targets. All three Piegan policemen were down, either dead or dying, the last two having been practically cut to ribbons by half-a-dozen bullets or more.

Longarm climbed to his feet and looked up toward the ridge he and the Piegan had vacated minutes earlier.

Tall Man showed himself on the skyline there. Tall Man and at least a dozen of his Crow warriors.

Under the circumstances, Longarm decided he would not complain about the Crow killing their old Piegan enemies, even if they were all supposed to be friends and neighbors nowadays.

No, sir, he wasn't going to fuss at them even a little bit for shooting down their agency neighbors like that.

Instead he pulled out a pair of rum crooks—he did wish Tall Man would get around to sharing some of those good cheroots he'd won off Longarm—and hoped he had enough of the vile things left in his saddlebags to properly reward the warriors Tall Man brought with him.

Chapter 34

"You already knew," Tall Man said, mouthing his words through a dense curtain of smoke from the crook Longarm had given him. Longarm thought the Crow sounded disappointed.

"I knew," Longarm agreed.

"How?"

"Same way I bet you figured it out. Short Tail Rabbit wasn't shot by accident from a distance. He couldn't have been mistaken for me and shot in my place. Whoever murdered him damn well intended to because they were standing not more than a few feet behind him. A heavy, slow-moving slug like one from a .50–70 rifle will only punch a hole at any range over fifty, sixty yards or so. In order to make as big as mess as Short Tail Rabbit's head was, the shooter had to be close enough to damn near tap him on the shoulder."

Tall Man grunted once and nodded, turning to repeat Longarm's words in his own language for the benefit of the other warriors.

"You did not need us as we thought you did."

"A man always needs his friends."

"But with these Piegan you did not need us," Tall Man said.

The truth was that Longarm had fully intended to take the Piegan alive if he could. He certainly had wanted at least one of them left alive and available for questioning.

That was no longer a possibility, however. Tall Man's Crow warriors had seen to that.

"What will you do now, Longarm?"

"I still need to speak with Cloud Talker."

"How will you find him?"

Longarm grinned. "That's another thing that was kinda a giveaway about those Piegan murderers. Usually, my friend, the most effective thing is also the simplest. To find Cloud Talker, I'll first go look for him at his lodge. If he isn't there, well, we'll worry about that if the time comes."

"Ha!" Tall Man barked. "Good. We will go with you."

"I'm not expecting trouble, Tall Man. Not from Cloud Talker."

"One never knows where trouble will find you. Or when."

"If you want to come along . . ."

"I will come."

Longarm grunted in agreement with the statement. It wasn't really a request. "After we see Cloud Talker, Tall Man, the three of us can go make sure there won't be any war between your people an' his."

"You know who killed the Piegan shaman and Short Tail Rabbit?"

"If you mean do I know yet exactly who it was that clubbed

164

John Jumps-the-Creek, no. I don't. Though when it comes to Short Tail Rabbit, I expect that the killer is lying on the ground over there. I don't think it really matters now which one of them killed him. The point is why they done it.''

"And you know the answer to this?" Tall Man asked.

Longarm sighed. Then shrugged. "Old friend, I don't have the faintest idea why all this has been done. I wish to hell I did, because then I think I could figure out all the other details that aren't lining up in my mind just yet.''

"We will go now. Talk to Cloud Talker." Tall Man stood, and his warriors sprang to their feet also.

Longarm glanced back at the bodies of the dead Piegan policemen. They probably ought to be given burials.

On the other hand . . . piss on them. What they already had was precisely what they deserved. If the Piegan wanted them properly buried, then the Piegan could come out and do the burying.

"Let's go, my friend."

Chapter 35

Cloud Talker wasn't exactly in hiding. The man was sitting outside his own lodge, cross-legged on a coyote skin, with a mirror in one hand and a pair of tweezers in the other, busy pulling stray whiskers off his face and neck. Longarm had seen Tall Man and others do the same thing many and many a time, and it purely hurt just to look at. A good razor and strop seemed mighty fine in comparison, and never mind the nuisance of having to shave so often.

Cloud Talker seemed surprised, and perhaps more than a little afraid as well, when he saw Tall Man and his band of Crow coming. Cloud Talker came to his feet and reached behind him for one of the ubiquitous Springfield rifles. "Does it start here, Long Arm? Have these enemies come to kill me?"

"They haven't come to kill you, Cloud Talker. And they aren't your enemies. Right now they could well be the closest thing you got to having friends. Have you heard about Short Tail Rabbit?"

"What of him?" Cloud Talker made his feelings on the subject clear enough. He turned his head and spat at the mention of his rival's name.

The Piegan shaman's attitude changed when he heard about the murder. A look of sharp alarm made his eye grow wide. But then, if the Piegan tribal police could murder Short Tail Rabbit, what would they do if they became angry with him as well.

"What does Agent MacNall say about this, Long Arm?"

"We haven't discussed it with him, Cloud Talker. We wanted to come see you first thing. Figured you, Tall Man, and me could all go see MacNall next an' see can we bring this mess to a conclusion everybody can live with."

"Yes, please. Whatever you say, Long Arm."

"Tell me something, though, Cloud Talker. Do you think you can control your tribal police? There's at least a few rogues runnin' with them."

"I . . . when the sun was young in the sky, Long Arm, I would have said to you that these men are Piegan. That they will follow me. But if what you say about Short Tail Rabbit is true. . . ."

"It's true enough, Cloud Talker," Longarm said.

"With my own eyes I saw the police try to shoot our friend in the back," Tall Man added. "If Longarm were not a warrior to be reckoned with, he would be dead now."

Cloud Talker shook his head. "I do not know. I do not know what to do now." He looked beyond Longarm, grimaced, and looked down toward the ground.

Longarm glanced around. The girl Angelica was there behind him. And the big white dog. For some reason Cloud Talker seemed unwilling to look at the girl.

"Hello," Longarm said. He smiled. "Do you know you're even prettier in daylight?"

Angelica ignored the flattery and approached Cloud Talker. She lightly touched Cloud Talker's forearm, a small gesture which aroused a pang of jealousy—stupid but undeniable—in Longarm's chest. Damn, the girl was gorgeous. She went way the hell past being merely pretty. She was so beautiful there ought to be, maybe was, a law against screwing her.

"You are a good man, Cloud Talker," she said. "But you are not your father. You cannot be shaman. Not such a one as he was."

"But you . . ."

Angelica nodded. "Yes. For our people."

Longarm realized that this, then, was the major battle for domination. Not between Cloud Talker and Short Tail Rabbit as he had thought. The larger confrontation had nothing to do with leadership in council. This, for the future of the Piegan tribe, was of much greater importance because this contest of wills to determine who would become shaman had to do with the tribe's health and their spiritual survival. And until now Longarm had not recognized either the importance of the choice . . . or who the players were.

"You ask too much," Cloud Talker said.

"I ask nothing for myself. It is the good of the people that I want. Can you say the same, Cloud Talker? Can you come with me to the high place to fast and seek the guidance of the spirits? Will you do that, Cloud Talker? Will you let the spirits choose between us?"

Cloud Talker winced. It was a challenge that a shaman could not duck. After a moment, thoroughly miserable, he nodded. "When this is done," he said. "We will go to the high place. We will fast. We will know the will of the spirits."

"That's good for the Piegan nation," Longarm put in, "but it doesn't do much to take care of the problem between you an' the Crow. There's still the renegade police to worry about an' the fact that so many of your people think the Crow killed John Jumps-the-Creek."

Angelica looked down at the dog, which had parked itself by Tall Man's ankles and was contentedly allowing the Crow chief to scratch its ears. "He likes you," she said.

Tall Man rubbed the dog's muzzle and said, "Fine dog. I would buy it. Use it to breed fat puppies."

"An' then put them into the stew pots," Longarm injected.

"Of course," Tall Man said. "What else?"

"He is a spirit wolf," Angelica said, "and he is not for sale."

"Tell me if you change your mind," Tall Man said.

"I will not change my mind."

Tall Man shrugged.

Longarm recalled that the girl had once said something about the dog—wolf, whatever—taking a part in this, but he couldn't remember what that was supposed to be about.

Nothing important, apparently. The creature looked like a happy, mild-tempered pet sitting there with its tongue lolling and eyes drooping sleepily while Tall Man continued to scratch and pet it.

"I think," Longarm said, "we should go talk to the Reverend MacNall an' see what he thinks we should do to get the police force cleaned up, an' see can we figure out who actually swung the club that killed John Jumps-the-Creek."

"You will know," Angelica said. She pointed off toward the sun, which was sinking inexorably toward the distant horizon. "Before the fire of the sun touches the hills to the west," Angelica said, "the murderer of the shaman will meet his death."

"You're sure of that?" Longarm asked. Angelica's prediction was bold, sure, but foolhardy. Whoever had killed the old shaman wasn't likely to jump up and shout out a confession. And the process of proving responsibility was apt to be a long and difficult one, even knowing full well who was ultimately responsible for the act.

"I am sure," Angelica said. "The spirits have told me. The spirits do not lie."

"If you say so. Tall Man? Cloud Talker? If you boys are ready, I think we'd best go now. Before, uh, sundown."

He glanced back at Angelica, but the pretty girl quite obviously was unaware of any sarcasm that might have been implied.

The small party set off on foot to accommodate Cloud Talker and Angelica, while several of the Crow warriors came along behind leading the horses.

Chapter 36

The usual group of Piegan tribal police was gathered outside the agency headquarters. Perhaps it was only his recent experience that was influencing Longarm, but he thought the whole damn bunch of them looked like a bunch of sullen, insolent thugs. The truth, of course, was that for all he really knew, these might be the best and the finest and the most honorable of all the Piegan warriors.

But then hopefully, that was one of the things that would soon be worked out.

There was no sign of the Reverend MacNall, but probably he was inside in conference with Captain Wingate. The army officer's horse was tied to the hitching rail close to where the police were squatting to smoke and swap lies.

When Longarm and the others arrived, the policemen stood and—not an entirely friendly gesture—reached for their Springfields. Longarm, Tall Man, and Cloud Talker confronted the policemen while the Crow warriors, perhaps thinking to avoid being taken as a threat, took the horses and went off toward the back of the headquarters.

"Where are the men who went with you?" a dark-skinned Piegan warrior with corporal's stripes on his sleeves asked in challenge.

"Dead," Longarm said.

"You murdered them?"

"No, but I sure as hell defended myself from 'em," Longarm answered. "I think you boys need some cleaning out, Corporal. Right quick."

The man's answer was to lift the muzzle of his .50–70 so the big rifle was aimed more or less in the direction of Longarm's belt buckle.

"I'm glad Colonel Wingate is here, Corporal. Him an' his soldiers will be taking over the duties of policing this agency while the tribal police are reorganized."

"You cannot—"

"But I can. I have the authority to do exactly that." Which was pushing the truth all it would stretch and then some, but somehow Longarm doubted that this Piegan police corporal was much of an authority on constitutional law.

"We will not let you."

"You got no choice about it, Corporal. The police force is disbanded as of right now. You and your boys lay down your rifles and . . . Corporal, if that thumb o' yours so much as comes close to the hammer on that rifle, you are gonna have yourself a fatal bellyache. I said—"

The corporal was not paying attention.

Or possibly the man had no idea just how fast a good man with a six-gun can put one into action.

The corporal jammed the hammer of his Springfield back to full cock.

And Longarm's first bullet hit him square in the chest—all right, so Longarm had lied about shooting him in the belly—at damn near the same instant.

The Piegan probably didn't even see the speed of the draw that killed him.

Behind the corporal the rest of the police were trying to get their guns into action.

One got a shot off, but it was high, ripping overhead somewhere between Longarm and Cloud Talker.

Longarm shot a private in the arm and another in the leg, and by then there were no good targets left because Tall Man's Crow warriors had posted themselves behind the Piegan and opened fire on the policemen at the signal of Longarm's first shot.

The Piegan crumpled and fell, and Tall Man and the other Crow were on them with hatchets and knives before the breath was out of them.

Blood and bits of flesh sprayed into the air and onto the side wall of the agency building. It was one ugly sonuvabitch of a sight, and the Crow continued to slash and hack and mutilate the police long after the men were dead.

The Reverend MacNall and his principal assistant, Charles Prandel, ran out onto the porch, but by then it was much too late for them to stop the butchery.

"My God, Long. Stop those men. Shoot them, arrest them, *some*thing!" MacNall yelled.

Longarm didn't see much point in trying. After all, the Piegan were already dead. Still, it was true that Cloud Talker looked mighty grieved. "Tall Man. Call your warriors off, will you?"

Tall Man seemed as intent as anyone on chopping policemen into pieces, but he heard and stopped whacking. He said something in his own language and after a moment, one by one, his warriors slowed their efforts and gradually quit.

By then there was more blood on the ground beside the agency building than one might find in a Chicago packinghouse. Or so it looked anyhow.

"What is the meaning of this, Marshal?" MacNall demanded.

"Retribution, I think you might say," Longarm told him. "An' justice." He glanced toward the west. Damned if the girl hadn't been right after all. The sun was just now approaching the horizon. "Your police have what you might call 'exceeded their authority' lately. Like committing murder."

"Why would they do that?"

"I ain't entirely for sure, Reverend," Longarm admitted. "I was hoping you could tell me that. I—"

A pale and deadly ghost-shape dashed in front of Longarm, moving so quickly it seemed a blur.

A flash of white. A menacing growl. A leap high into the air.

Reverend MacNall threw a hand up in a vain attempt to block the fangs from his face.

The white dog—Angelica's so-called spirit wolf—hit the agent full in the chest and sent him crashing backward, onto the floor and hard against the wall.

MacNall screamed as the dog bit and tore at his flesh.

Longarm could have shot the animal. Probably should have shot it. His .44 was already in his hand and the dog was less than a dozen paces distant, its back to him and all its attention concentrated on savaging the Indian agent.

Longarm could have shot it. Except his hand remained motionless even while he gave thought to the need to defend MacNall.

174

He stood there and watched as the dog slashed and snarled.

He continued to stand there, rooted and immobile, as the dog ripped Ames MacNall's throat out and shook the dying man like a terrier shakes a rat.

And he continued to stand in awe as the dog backed away from the body of its victim, shook itself once, and then calmly trotted off the porch and out of sight around the back of the building.

"The sun is now touching the far hills, Longarm," Cloud Talker said softly.

Longarm shook himself and looked around. Angelica was gone. So was the dog. The spirit wolf. Longarm felt a chill dance up his spine.

Over on the porch Charles Prandel stood trembling with fear, his forehead beaded with cold sweat.

"I think," Longarm said, "we got to ask you some questions, Prandel. I think . . ."

"Longarm."

"Yes, Tall Man?"

Tall Man and one of his warriors were standing in the entrance to the headquarters. Longarm hadn't so much as noticed them go inside, but probably they had gone looking to see if there were any more Piegan police who needed killing. A chore which none of the Crow seemed to find all that distasteful, actually.

"The captain, Wingate, Longarm."

"Yes?"

"He is in here. He has been bound with handcuffs and gagged, Longarm. You should come, I think."

"Yeah, I reckon I should at that. Cloud Talker, you watch Prandel there. Don't let him go anyplace, hear?"

Longarm holstered his Colt and stepped wide around the gore that marked the Reverend MacNall's death.

Chapter 37

"Greed," Wingate said. The officer was seated behind Ames MacNall's desk, the Indian agent's records spread out before him. The documents might as well have been written in Piegan for all Longarm understood them, but to Wingate they were clear as Austrian crystal. "MacNall and his friend Prandel there have been making a fortune off their assignment at this agency." Wingate rubbed his wrists where the steel of the manacles had chafed and gouged him.

"You say you already suspected it?" Longarm asked.

The officer nodded. "That's what brought me here this afternoon. I wanted to call MacNall to account for his excesses. Do you remember that I had a load of goods delivered to Camp Beloit recently?"

"Sure. You said you had to check it all in, I believe. What'd they do, short the amounts on you an' hold stuff back for themselves to sell on the side?"

"Oh, much more lucrative than anything that simple. And

in fact, the amounts delivered were exactly as invoiced." Wingate gave Prandel a tight smile that held no mirth whatsoever. Prandel was seated nearby, wearing the handcuffs recently removed from Wingate's wrists.

"I imagine they expected me to verify the amounts of goods, as of course I did. But what they did not anticipate was that I would also know what they paid for each of those items.

"Longarm, for the past eight years I have sat behind a desk supervising the granting of contracts for procurement and haulage at frontier posts from the north of Dakota Territory to the southern tip of Arizona Territory. I know the contract rates. I know what each hundredweight of flour costs, every bottle of vinegar or slab of bacon. I can tell you off the top of my head the freight charges of the twenty leading transportation contractors west of the Mississippi River. And I could see at a glance the profits MacNall and this man were raking in by falsely reporting their costs and pocketing the difference.

"I haven't confirmed all of it in these books. Yet. But I can tell you that they have been stealing from the government at a rate that I expect will total in the tens of thousands each year."

"Just that easy?" Longarm asked.

"Just that easy," Wingate said. "It is quite simple, of course. They bought bacon, for instance, at three cents per pound, but charged against the agency accounts at the rate of five cents."

"Fine, but two lousy cents . . ."

"Adds up to a great deal of money when you are thinking in terms of tons upon tons of supplies of various sorts. Beef, flour, blankets—why, they even drew funds at the rate of three quarters of a cent per cartridge for ammunition for all those rifles they said they bought at two dollars and a half apiece.

And the quartermaster to my certain knowledge delivered the rifles and the ammunition without charge other than the transportation.''

"They figured to get rich," Longarm said.

"Figured, hell, Longarm, they *were* getting rich."

"Which explains why they grabbed you and were fixing to kill you this afternoon. But why John Jumps-the-Creek? I mean, the old boy was a friend of mine. He was a great shaman and a leader of his people. But he didn't know or care a damn thing about logistics or the cost of things.''

"I think he did care about the welfare of his people, though," Wingate said.

"That he did, I guarantee it. He was a genuinely good man, and would never have let anything bad happen to the Piegan nation. Not if he had any say in the matter.''

"Could he have kept the Piegan from going to war with the Crow?''

"Yes, I think John Jumps-the-Creek was strong enough to do that," Longarm answered.

"You should probably ask your friend there"—Wingate pointed toward Charles Prandel—"but I think I know what MacNall had in mind. The same reason why he had his political cronies back in Washington have an ineffective field officer assigned to command Camp Beloit, actually.''

"I don't understand," Longarm admitted.

"MacNall and Prandel, along with whoever else they were paying off in this deal, wanted to reduce the population of the agency. They wanted me here because they were sure a desk officer like me would not be able to stop the hostilities MacNall himself intended to generate.''

"But . . .''

"It makes sense, Longarm, when you look at the cold figures on paper. It costs roughly seven dollars . . . six dollars and fifty-four cents if you want to draw a fine line . . . to feed and clothe one agency Indian, Crow or Piegan, for one month. MacNall was drawing funds at the rate of approximately twelve dollars per Indian per month.''

"Giving him one helluva nice profit,'' Longarm said.

"But not enough to satisfy his dark soul, I think. By killing off, say, two hundred people . . . and then not reporting those losses to the Department of the Interior . . . he could reap the full twelve dollars per head instead of a meager five, as he was already doing.''

"Jesus,'' Longarm blurted out.

"I somehow doubt the reverend took Jesus into account when he was making his plans,'' Wingate said dryly.

"Do you have enough evidence that we can convict Prandel of all this?''

"There is certainly enough to have convicted MacNall, but that is moot now. I think . . . no, I think there will not be sufficient evidence to charge Mr. Prandel.''

"Then what do you think I should do with him?'' Longarm asked.

Wingate smiled. "I think we have no choice in the matter, Longarm. We will have to turn him loose. Why don't you inform Cloud Talker and his Piegans of that. They might, um, wish to escort Mr. Prandel off the agency.''

"You can't do that!'' Prandel yelped. "You can't turn me over to those fucking savages. My God, man, you seen what they done to MacNall and the coppers. They'd do the same to me.''

"Sorry, man, but we can't possibly hold you without evidence against you.''

"I . . . I can give you evidence. A statement. A confession.

179

I'll sign anything you say. But don't turn me out for the Injuns to get at.''

Longarm stood and reached for a cigar. It seemed that L. Thompson Wingate had things rather nicely under control here. From this point on it was all paperwork anyway. And paperwork was exactly Wingate's meat.

Longarm wandered out into the cool of the evening. Tall Man and Cloud Talker had gone home, each in his own direction. There would be no trouble between their people now, Longarm was sure.

And if there were any more renegade Piegan of the sort who would put personal interests ahead of the good of the tribe, Longarm was sure the new Piegan leaders—whoever they turned out to be—would handle it without interference from the United States government.

In the meantime there was someone Longarm wanted to see once more before he left.

He found the chestnut horse tied at the rail next to Wingate's army mount and swung into the saddle.

''The girl you seek is not here, Long Arm. She has gone to fast and to speak with the spirits.''

''Thank you, Bad Tooth. Do you think she will be gone very long?''

''She will not return until Long Arm has returned to his own people. I am sorry, Long Arm, but Angelica said I should tell this to you. She will not see you again. There was something . . . a temptation? She did not explain this to me, but I know her. She is afraid to see you again. I do not know why.''

Longarm knew. It was a compliment that she would not see him again. It was a source of great sorrow as well.

The truth, though, was that Angelica loved her people far

more than she could ever love Longarm. Or any other mortal man.

And perhaps that was just as well, considering.

"Thank you, Grandmother. I have no presents for you and Juanita Maria tonight, but I will leave something for you at the agency. Please forgive me for not bringing anything tonight."

"It is not the presents that make you welcome here, Long Arm. You know this is true."

"Yes, I do, Grandmother." Longarm turned to leave, then remembered something and turned back to the old woman. "Bad Tooth."

"Yes, Long Arm?"

"Where is the white dog?"

"White dog, Long Arm?"

"Yes, the one that knew Ames MacNall was the man who murdered your husband."

Bad Tooth looked puzzled still.

"Don't you remember, Grandmother? When we talked before, Juanita Maria mentioned going outside and finding the dogs standing watch over your husband's body. Your big white dog must have been one of them."

"Yes, I remember when she said this, Long Arm. But . . . we have no white dog. We have never had a white dog. Brown, black, spotted, you have eaten of our dogs many times before now . . . but no, we have never had a white dog."

"But . . . the dog Angelica called the spirit wolf . . ."

Bad Tooth shrugged. "I am sorry, Long Arm. Not here."

Longarm turned and—unsure of just what to believe . . . or disbelieve—rode into the night.